Starlight and Moonshine

Also by Joseph O'Malley

Great Escapes from Detroit (stories)

Starlight and Moonshine

a novel

Joseph O'Malley

Delphinium Books

STARLIGHT AND MOONSHINE

Printed in the United States of America

For information, address DELPHINIUM BOOKS
1250 4th Street, 5th Floor
Santa Monica, California 90401

Library of Congress Catalog-in-Publication Data is available on request.
ISBN 978-1-953002-61-7

Jacket and interior design by Colin Dockrill, AIGA

For My Family

The Detroit News
Tuesday, March 25, 1980

Woman Killed in Crash on Northwest Side

A 45-year-old female driver of a white-topped, blue Plymouth Valiant crashed through a cyclone fence and into a large elm tree in front of a house on the corner of Outer Drive and Lahser Road Monday evening on Detroit's northwest side. The driver was pronounced dead on arrival at Mount Carmel Hospital.

Preliminary autopsy results showed a blood alcohol level of 0.3%, which is three times the legal limit in Michigan. "We are not releasing any names at this time because the accident is still under investigation," said Sixteenth Precinct Police Lieutenant Daniel Clemens.

Witnesses say the driver lost control of the car, ran a red light, then slammed through the fence and into the tree. Elaine Kadzjelowski, the resident of the home, said the elm was over 150 years old and badly scarred from two previous crashes, but otherwise structurally sound. “It’s a dangerous corner because of the curve. That’s why we put up the fence. But I suspect that tree will outlive us all,” said Mrs. Kadzjelowski. No one else was injured in the crash.

The Detroit News
Wednesday, March 26, 1980

Obituary

Fallon (née Grace), Hannah. Age 45. Died suddenly March 24, 1980. Dear wife of James Fallon. Beloved mother of Mary, Colleen, and Jack Fallon. Sister-in-law of Adelaide Fallon. Visitation Thursday 12 noon–8 p.m. Rosary at 6:30 p.m. at RG and GR McAlpine Funeral Home, Redford. Funeral Mass Friday 9:00 a.m. at St. Benedict's Catholic Church, Detroit. Internment Holy Sepulchre Cemetery.

Maintenance

Stitched in white letters on the navy blue shirt I wear to work at Sinai Hospital is the word "Maintenance," which rests on my chest over the pocket where I clip my ID badge. The beige walls in the west wing of the hospital have a wide orange stripe running along them about three feet above the floor. At Employee Orientation they said if I see visitors walking around with a blue, red, or yellow visitor's pass in the orange section of the hospital, I'm supposed to help them find where they need to go.

I clean SICU, the Surgical Intensive Care Unit, an open unit with twelve patient rooms, six on one side, six on the other. In the center of the unit sits a raised platform with a desk, telephones, and monitors. Sandy, Adrienne, Rachel, and Lynn are the regular day shift nurses, and everyone calls me Jack except for Lynn, a pale wiry woman whose thin mouth turns down even when she smiles. She insists on calling me Maintenance, as if the letters on my shirt blocked out the name on my ID badge. Sandy, the charge nurse, is blond and funny. Adrienne is short with a round face and an Irish accent, and Rachel is a tall, dark-haired woman who tells everyone she loves the term "Jewess." Ms. Sheffield is the full-time floor clerk, a large, happy woman with light brown skin and a shiny face. She answers the phone, shuffles the papers that need to be shuffled, organizes and orders everything that needs to be done, and tells the nurses and doctors what they need to know. Sometimes she also tells them more than they need to know, like "Your hair look good today!" or "That doctor's an asshole, pay him no never mind," just a little something extra to make the work day flow steady and sure.

SICU takes most of my shift's eight hours to clean, but it's worth it. When I look back at a room, it shines with clean. My clean.

My sister Mary is unpacking groceries from her car when I get home from work. Thin as she is, her skirt stretches to the limit every time she bends to pick up another bag. She's studying at Henry Ford Community College because the basic liberal art credits are cheaper. She says she'll study art history or nursing when she transfers to the university. Colleen, who is older than I am, but younger than Mary, should be home by six thirty. She's on the waiting list for the Culinary Arts program at Schoolcraft College, so she works at the bank to save for tuition. Mary manages a bakery part-time to make money.

I don't know what I'm doing. Ten months ago in the waning light of a March evening, our mother drove home drunk, careening down Outer Drive on the night of the winter's last big snow. She twisted the car, herself, a cyclone fence, and part of an elm tree into a hard, sprawling mess at the end of my senior year in high school. After that, the pale walls at school, the drab lockers, the gray cement all chipped and broken out in front of the school, the sound of the traffic on Grand River Avenue, even the beige and black tile floors made me clench, so I stopped going. Dad suggested I get a job at the Detroit Salt Mine. "Probably decent pay," he said. "Benefits." In the days when Dad would hold both my hands and spin around on the front lawn until my feet left the ground while Mom, Colleen, and Mary watched and I almost peed myself from laughing, Mom and Dad would tell us of the glorious city of salt beneath Detroit and how they went on their first date at the salt mine.

But that was a long time ago. I told Dad I couldn't work at a mine. I need to stay aboveground.

Dad's friend told him of a job at Sinai Hospital, so I called and called. They finally hired me after I told them I'd go to night school at Schoolcraft to get my GED. We sat with the desks in a circle at Schoolcraft, the room all lit up at night where I could see my reflection in the window, and then I didn't mind school so much. Now I tell anyone who asks that I'm working to save money for college, because it makes people more comfortable when they think they're talking to someone with a plan.

I walk up the driveway past Mary and she says, "How's our Jack?" putting a bag into my arms. She's wearing only a jean jacket with a light purple scarf of Mom's tied loosely around her neck. She's dressed for another date tonight.

I say, "You'll freeze your arse off like that." She smirks, pats my head like I'm her puppy. I like that. I set the bag on the kitchen table, then go take my nap.

Most nights it's just me, Mary, and Colleen. My high school friends have moved away to college in Ann Arbor, Kalamazoo, Lansing, or Mount Pleasant. Dad's been disappearing for a long time. Dad's sister, Adelaide, comes over to "check in" on us, she says, but really she comes to eat our food and take home the leftovers. She's alone except for us. A few years ago I overheard Ma telling someone on the phone that Adelaide once told Dad that if he married Ma, she'd never speak to him again. I guess Aunt Addy changed her mind, since she's eaten dinner at our house at least three nights of every week for as long as

I can remember. Between bites of Ma's food, she'd say things like, "There was no cook like my mother, nor ever will be," or "Hannah, you could take a lesson from my friend Rita's hamburger. I'll get you the recipe."

Dad hasn't come home before midnight since the end of summer. He gets up at five thirty to take his shower so I can take mine at six. He's an electrician at Greenfield Village, but he doesn't start until eight. We have no idea where he goes so early or stays so late. He's always had moods where he'd stow himself in the basement workroom and hammer away all alone, but that usually had to do with a spat he'd had with Ma or something, and she was always able to pull him back into our orbit. Without Ma, Dad is free floating.

We never have to ask him for anything. He pays the bills and lets us live here. He leaves money on the kitchen table for groceries. None of us has ever had an allowance, and we all work anyway, so there's no desire for anything, and that's fine with me.

Aunt Addy tells us not to ask him about it. She knows her brother and it's best not to pick. "Your mother picked at him all the time. It'll just drive him further away," she once said. She sits in her usual spot at the kitchen table and tells us what to do while Colleen makes dinner. "Be tough," she says. "It's a hard world."

"Bullshit," Colleen tells her tonight as she sets

Aunt Addy's plate down in front of her. "We're all happy here, aren't we?"

"You remind me so much of your mother," Aunt Addy says through a little laugh, and begins to eat.

Mary says, "Jack, did you see what Aunt Addy brought Colleen?" She sets a white plastic thing on the table, but I can't figure out what I'm looking at. I touch the rim of it with two fingers, say, "Oh," and smile at Aunt Addy.

"It's for the washroom," Aunt Addy says. "I got it for Colleen, but everyone can enjoy it. It's a radio, but it also holds toilet paper rolls. Because Colleen's so musical."

Colleen sets down a bowl of red sauce on the table, and sits with us. "Help yourselves to more sauce," she says. "Sometimes the baking dries out the lasagna."

Addy says, "Know what I think? I think you should stay at that bank and forget this nonsense about cooking school. You already know how to cook." She nods and turns her head as if it's on a swivel to look at me and Mary. "It doesn't take that much sense."

Colleen chews her food slowly.

Between forkfuls of Colleen's lasagna, Aunt Addy points her stubby finger at me. "And what about you? You can't clean toilets your whole life, Jack."

When I work in SICU, I only have three toilets to

clean. When I work on one of the Internal Medicine nursing floors that flank SICU, I have at least thirty. I transform what people find disgusting into something extraordinarily clean. Yes, toilets are dirty. But then you wash and disinfect them. You can see the clean. Sanitation is something I know for sure. So I think: Why not? Why can't I clean toilets my whole life? Toilets have to be cleaned. Why not by me, someone who cares?

Except for a Vietnam vet named Gary and a retarded guy named Owen, I'm the only white guy in the department. This seems to matter to people. Other departments at Sinai have more of a mix. A lot of older Jewish women visitors look at the white stitching on my uniform, then at my face, and take me to the side. "You're in school . . ." they begin, lipstick bleeding into the cracks around their mouths. Some people think they have the right to say anything to me just because I'm young and white and work a mop.

Most of the ladies in Maintenance are between forty and sixty years old and range in color from butter to coffee bean. They take breaks and lunch together, sit around and talk about their babies or their grandbabies. They call me baby too. "Hey, baby, how you doing today?" Or they'll talk about me to someone else in front of me: "That child is so peaceful," Lois might say. "Mmm-hhmmm," chimes in Evelyn, "never bothers nobody."

There were more people my age working in the summer, but now that it's January, I only see a handful, mostly on weekends and holidays, and they usually sit together for lunch and breaks. I've never been one to foist myself onto a group without being asked, so I was glad when Hector asked if he could sit at my table. I had seen him making rounds with the wire pharmacy cart he pushes around the hospital to deliver baggies of prepackaged pills, big plastic and glass containers of IV fluids to the floors. His voice is low and smooth, and when he talks, his *s*'s and *l*'s ride over his tongue and teeth with a strange reverberation inside the words. He has a clean, crooked smile that turns up on the left, and he has flashed it hello at me a couple times while passing through SICU. That first day, he took off his short blue lab coat before he sat down. The tan skin of his thick arms stood out against the white of his short-sleeved shirt. Suddenly the dark blue shirt I wear made my arm seem skinnier and more pale than ever, even under long sleeves. Another pharmacy technician named Carmelita, Charles from Phlebotomy, Cherie from Patient Transport, and Etienne from Dietary also joined us. They're all students at Wayne State University. When I gave them my line about saving money for school, I saw

Carmelita's jaw relax into a smile.

"Anytime you want to go downtown to check out the campus," Hector said to me in front of everyone, "just let me know. You can come with me to look around."

"Thanks," I said. I scratched at a clump of dried egg left on the table from the morning and waited for someone else to start talking.

About two hours after I'd get home from school every day, Mom would waltz into the house, flip on the stereo in the living room, and spread the cookbooks out on the kitchen table. She'd pour her first glass of red wine and dance around with it, singing along to Blossom Dearie, Joni Mitchell, Nina Simone, Eartha Kitt. Even Astrud Gilberto during the English parts. Mom was a rotten singer, with a wet, croaky voice, and I think she knew it, but sang anyway more for the feeling of it in her throat than the sound she made. By the time we'd finished supper every night, she was whipped. "I think I'll take a nap," she'd say. The rest of us would fight about who would do the dishes, and we wouldn't see her again until the next day.

She worked as a secretary at St. Benedict's Elementary School, a job she got when Mary, Colleen, and I were students there. The lay teachers befriended her right away. She went out for drinks with them every so often after school and got the skinny on the nuns: for example, how Sister Philomena, Polish and ancient, had probably become a nun to avoid going into a concentration camp; how Sister Evangelista came from a famous Mafia family; and how Sister Virginia joined the order after giving her illegitimate baby up for adoption. Ma told us all of this at the dinner table years after we'd gone on to high school.

In our house, every holiday was a feast, even the holidays no one paid attention to: St. Blaise Day, the Feast of the Assumption, Groundhog Day. "Experimentation, Jack," she'd say. "Experiment or live a long, slow death." We had jerk pork, falafel, borscht, shepherd's pies, risottos, saganaki, latkes, egg drop soup, dishes from every edge of the world. Our friends constantly tried to finagle dinner invitations, so she always made extra, just in case.

Right before dinner, we'd set the table around Dad as he sat in his spot doing his crossword puzzle. Mom would put the garlic bread in the oven, asking us to watch that one last thing while she took a shower. She'd pour the last of the bottle into her wineglass, come to the table smelling of shampoo, her thick straight hair still wet, the color of an old well-spent penny with one shock of silver coming in above her left ear. That's how I think of her, looking a bit tired with her red eyes, maybe even a little embarrassed to be enjoying herself, her family, the food, the wine.

Death is so dramatic, you can't help but wish there was something different about the particular day it happens to someone you know: a fight, a rush to get somewhere, some emotional push in the wrong direction. Because you want death to be special, don't you? If it's just something normal that happens all the time, that happens to everybody, then you're left with no reason. The day Mom died, everything was normal. Alive, then dead. That's it. Nothing special really, when you think about it.

I have a system. I clean the nurses' dressing room and all patient rooms in SICU daily. Room 1 is directly across from Room 12, Room 2 across from 11, and so on. I start at the east end in Rooms 1 and 12 and work my way west through the unit. I have a steel cart with a small bucket on top, two shelves of supplies underneath, and mop bucket and mop on the side. I write down the room numbers on a piece of paper towel and cross the number off when I finish a room. If a nurse is working with a patient and I can't get in or finish the room, then I circle the number, or write "sink done" next to it if that's all I've done, or "floor" if that's all I have left to do, so I don't forget to come back.

Rose Schwartz is a surgical accident, a huge lawsuit against the hospital, and therefore a permanent SICU resident in Room 1. Hers is always the first room I clean. Rose's eyes never open; her hands are cramped like claws, as are her feet. She lies in bed and cries an incessant song of "Oy! Oy! Oy! Oy!" while awake. When I clean Rose's room, I softly sing her name over and over between the oys, *Rose Rose Rose*, so only she can hear.

I sweep the room with long, even strokes of a dry cloth mop, move debris carefully so as not to stir the dust. If dust floats up and spreads itself around, it can infect a fresh surgical wound. Colored plastic covers popped off the tops of tubing and IV sets, swabs of cotton that have missed the trash bin, bits of paper towel and paper wrappings torn off sterilized equipment are strewn throughout the room. I collect it all into a neat clump that sweeps up easily once I'm outside the room.

I rub the sink clean, scrub the wall, the tall plastic wastebasket. Gunk and body fluids often leak through the garbage bags into the basket. I scour the filth away, make sure the wastebasket smells fresh before I return it double lined with heavy-duty bags to the patient's room. If the sharps container is filled with needles, I secure it, remove it, and replace it with a new empty one. There must be enough antibacterial soap and paper towels to last until I return the next day. My special touch: A bottle of hand lotion next to the sink prevents chapped hands on the nurses.

Then I mop. Unlike other commercial cleansers that smell of chlorine or ammonia or some other smell that scrapes the inside of your nose, Sanifresh has a scent like Castile soap, the soothing smell of a bath at home in your own tub. I change the water every two or three rooms, depending on how dirty a room is, or if there's blood or vomit or sputum or excrement of any sort. In which case I'll change it right away.

I have to be careful not to knock down IV poles or snag a line in the web of tubes, plugs, and wires that stretch taut between the machines, the walls, and the patient.

If I have time, I sweep and mop the whole unit from east to west.

That's a normal day with no interruptions, but there's always something: A nurse dropping a bottle that spews glass or some fluid, medical or hazardous, over the floor. Or a particularly bad patient.

One time Sandy asked me to clean Room 3, but barely looked at me when she spoke. The yellow cloth curtain muffled the voices coming from the room, and the floor just outside the curtain was covered with bloody footprints. "We're not ready for you yet," Sandy said, "but be prepared, we'll need the room cleaned quickly before we bring in the family." Rachel and Adrienne came out of the room and asked if I had an extra bucket they could use to wipe down the bed before the husband came in. Because of a strange chemical reaction, blood turns diluted Sanifresh, which is normally clear and yellow, a dark green. When they finally called me, I had to change my bucket three times. The patient was completely covered with a fresh sheet. The nurses talked to each other as if I wasn't there. A twenty-eight-year-old woman was walking through the shopping mall in the morning with her husband when she began to bleed. She was six months pregnant. Something detached. They tried to find out what was happening, but couldn't stop the bleeding. Four hours later, at two o'clock in the afternoon, I was mopping the floor under her bed while nurses and doctors discussed what to say when they told her husband that wife and baby were gone. Snap, just like that.

I made that room as clean as I could so when he came in to touch his wife's body one last time, he wouldn't know the full horror. It was all I could do for that poor man. Don't tell me what I do isn't important.

When I get home, Mary isn't here. Normally she's got her books stretched across the kitchen table, studying, but today I have the house to myself. I know I will have a sound nap. Colleen comes in at six thirty and I help her with dinner. At nine o'clock Mary walks in pale and pissed while we're playing a game of Rummy at the kitchen table.

"What's with you?" Colleen asks, fingers disappearing into her curly auburn hair.

"After school I was going to go shopping at Fairlane," Mary says, "but on the way, I saw Dad's car, so I followed him."

Colleen crosses her arms, squeezing out a sound somewhere between a sigh and a whistle. A pad of flesh pouches out under her chin when she looks at the floor, much the way her breasts balloon up against her crossed arms. She's never been as thin as Mary, but suddenly I see how much weight she's gained since the funeral.

Mary tells us, "I wanted to see where he goes instead of coming home."

Even though I tell myself I don't care, I ask, "Where'd he go?"

Mary has a long hank of curly black hair that she plays with when she gets nervous. She pulls the hair over her shoulder and twists it in both hands while she talks, blue eyes blazing.

"I followed him into the parking lot of the Detroit Race Course. I would've just left when I saw him get out of the car, but he had something in his hand, and I was too curious. I wanted to see what he was up to. I walked in behind him, trying to keep him from seeing me. I got into the line next to his because it was about five people longer, then I figured, shit, if he sees me, so what? I didn't even care anymore. If he's going to gamble away all our money, I have a right to know. He put ten dollars on a horse in the next race, then went up to the lounge. He didn't even see me. Walked right past."

"What *lounge*?" says Colleen like she's spitting out a bad piece of meat.

Mary puckers her mouth. "They have a dining lounge that looks out over the track," Mary says, "and you can eat there or drink while you watch the race. He watched the first race, got some dinner and a glass of wine . . ."

"One?" says Colleen.

"One, and he'd only drunk half of it by the time I left. Anyway, he ate dinner, then read the rest of the time. He barely looked at the track and never placed another bet. That's what he had in his hand, a book."

"What was he reading?" I ask.

"What difference does it make? It was just a stupid book. I watched him for half an hour, then I couldn't stand it anymore. I tapped him on the shoulder, and when he turned and saw it was me, he didn't even seem surprised. Like we meet there all the time, and I was late or something."

"What'd he say?"

"Nothing."

"Well, what did you say?"

"I just . . . I asked him what was going on. He said it was warm there, and quiet, and that he liked to go there to be alone. 'Where I don't have to talk to anyone,' he said."

"Not even us?" Colleen says.

"That's what I said." He just smiled that tired smile he has and held up his book. 'You should probably go home and study,' he said. I got the message. He's probably still there."

Colleen, exasperated, says, "Jesus. And you just left? Well, now that we know where he goes, I'll go tomorrow and talk to him."

Mary and I both laugh. "Now that we know where he goes, he'll never go there again," Mary says. "Plus, he lives here. We could all wait up and talk to him here. Maybe Aunt Addy's right. We should just leave him alone. It's not like he's done anything wrong."

We're all quiet for a minute, then Mary says, "That's what pisses me off. He hasn't done anything wrong that we know of, but he avoids us like he has, so we doubt him. And then I'm ashamed of myself."

"Don't be stupid," says Colleen. "We've done nothing to be ashamed of."

"And yet," says Mary, "I am."

"I can't believe you didn't see what book it was." I get up from the table and go upstairs into Dad's room to look around. Mary follows me, and Colleen screams after us, "We're playing a game here! Jack. Remember?"

"I'm winning anyway," I say.

"You stop, and I win," she says.

"Fine," I shout from the stairs that lead up to the bedroom, "you win."

The bed is in the corner. Some dirty clothes hang limply over the edges of a pale blue laundry basket near the closet. On a pair of Dad's navy blue work pants, the hem of one leg is frayed; the extra material hangs down in a jagged tatter. He was always very neat about his clothes and made sure we were too, but lately he's threadbare and ruffled. Just last week Colleen had to sew up a hole under his work jacket arm, then yesterday I saw a tuft of white stuffing poke out of the seam of his pocket. His bed is neatly made, and somehow this comforts me.

Built into the wall, a short, long bookshelf holds a few hundred books, which we look through searching for something, but we don't know what. *Moby Dick* leans against *Great Expectations*. A biography of

Maria Callas rests on top of Shakespeare. These were Mom's. Some books I remember having to read in high school, but most I have never heard of. A few pages are dog-eared, and some have lines or whole passages underlined, or notes in Mom's skinny handwriting. Next to a paragraph in *Emma*, it says: *So mean!* In *Lolita*, she has written on a page: *mouth? other parts?!!* We spend an hour or so reading, searching. Sometimes you'll do anything to find an answer, but it helps to have a clear question first. We don't. In the end, our search doesn't tell us anything.

I'm a half hour late for work this morning because every time I stop the car at a traffic light, it stalls. It's the weekend, and SICU has emptied out. Evelyn and Lois have a ton of discharges on the Internal Medicine floors, so I help them. They are a natural pair. Evelyn's skin is almost as light as mine, but she has large dark freckles that cover her nose and cheeks. Lois has smooth, dark velvety brown skin. She's short and thick and moves slowly but talks so fast, sometimes I have a hard time understanding her. Evelyn's hands and thin body move quickly from task to task, but her voice is almost slower than Lois's walk.

I help Evelyn first, and when we're done, we walk over to help Lois. Evelyn has two sons, one who became a dentist, and another who is in jail. Lois's daughter began law school this year in Chicago. Lois is a little sad, but says, "What's best is best. This is best, but I miss her fierce."

Both of them get on me about when am I going to start school. Lois has finished scrubbing the bathroom, and now she's wiping down the nightstand while Evelyn and I wash the plastic-covered mattress and the bed.

"This is no way to live, Jack. Working in other people's dirt. Getting paid pittance," says Lois. Evelyn nods in agreement as Lois talks, occasionally throwing in a "Yes," or an "I know that's right."

"Smart boy like you," says Lois, "need to make your momma proud."

"SShhhht, Lois," says Evelyn in her drawl. "Jack, you do it for you. I know it's hard, and you probably think you don't need advice from some old woman, but I know." She holds the folded mattress back while I wipe down the wire bedsprings with Sanifresh. "I know this much," she says. "I cleaned beds and washed toilets twenty-five years now, and this is no way"—she pauses—"no way to live." The bed is really dusty. I have to rinse my rag two or three times while they talk. "My babies are all grown now," she says, "and the one came up good, thank the Lord, but the other. Well." She stops and shakes her head while she looks past me out the window at the traffic. "I don't do this because I like it, you know. There are plenty other things I'd like to be doing."

"I don't mind this," I say.

Evelyn rests a hand on the bed, stares at me hard. She turns her attention to the mattress with her other hand, and it seems she's scrubbing out her sentences. "But you're living at home now," she says. "You can save money. You have choices. Choices. I suppose there are worse things to do, but with school you might be able to get something that lets you live. Do better for yourself. And one day, you never know, you might be doing for someone else too."

"It's just me," I say.

"You go to school and get yourself a job with good money," fires Lois. She's sitting in the corner now, her arms limp over the sides of the chair. "Life's hard enough, you never know what'll happen."

"I heard that," says Evelyn. She stands up straight, puts both fists at the small of her back, and stretches. "Mm-hmm. I surely did hear that."

I'm back in SICU finishing up near Rose's room when Hector comes by on his pharmacy round and asks me what's up for my weekend. I tell him about my car, and he says it sounds like the carburetor. He has no plans for tonight either, so he offers to look at it after work. I get out at three thirty and he finishes at four. I punch out at the time clock just outside the maintenance supervisor's office in the basement, follow the orange stripe past the red stripe near the pharmacy, and I wait for Hector on the first floor in the main blue lobby, where I watch the visitors mill around waiting for their relatives or news of some sort. I can't tell what they're feeling, who is sad, who is happy, they all look the same.

I follow Hector to his house in my car. Once we're on the highway, it's okay, but it still takes over an hour because I keep stalling at the traffic lights near the hospital and in his neighborhood. Hector talks to his parents in Spanish, his father laughs a lot, saying whatever he's saying to Hector, moving his hands up and down and cutting the air into consecutive segments with the edge of his hand.

The garage has enough space for a car and a wooden work bench with lots of tools. I drive the car onto two wooden ramps that his father made. We put a dirty blanket on the cold oily cement underneath the car. I don't understand anything about cars, but I try to help Hector twist and pull at the gadgets under the hood. "It could be something else besides the carburetor too," says Hector, so we lie on the blanket side by side and peek and poke and wipe from various angles at the curling pipes and tubes and wires. Hector explains what he's doing, telling me the names of things and what they do, but I can't concentrate and don't remember any of it.

By about nine o'clock, he somehow knows it's fixed, so we take it for a ride around his neighborhood. I've never seen this part of Detroit before. All the store signs are in Spanish. Hector asks me if I like burritos and takes me to a place where he orders for both of us in Spanish. He gets root beer, I get orange juice, and we take it back to eat in his garage. We're so hungry, we peel back the aluminum foil and eat the burritos before we even attempt to clean up, grease from the car all over our hands, the smell of oil threatening to ruin the taste, but somehow it doesn't. Maybe it's because I'm starving, but the burrito is really hot and tastes better than anything Colleen or Mom has ever made.

After we straighten up the garage, put the tools back where they belong, Hector brings out a large jar of white goop to clean the grease off our hands.

"This works better than anything," he says, "and it doesn't smell bad either."

He dips his hands in the goop. His greasy fingers leave behind a trail. The goop smells slightly like oranges.

"Here," he says, and takes one of my hands. "You have to rub hard." He slathers the slimy stuff all over, rubbing especially hard in places where the grease is caked, my thumb, knuckles, fingertips, even the palm of my hand and my wrists, although there isn't much grease there. The white goop turns gray, then black with grease, and drips down onto the light gray cement between us.

"I can do it," I say, and I take back my hands. For a long time we're both silent, listening to the liquid squish. Hector gets a roll of paper towels from the corner of the work bench to dry his hands. When he's done, he takes my hands again and wipes them off, and I let him. We're both looking at my white skin against his brown. We are completely clean. All it takes is a little tug from him and I'm right there. We're the same height. His eyes are brown. He tastes like hot sauce and root beer.

Something goes "clang," probably a metal can condensing in the cold night air, and I pull away first, my hand pressing on his shoulder. I don't know where to look. No, I think. Not this. Not yet. And though my feet are cold and I'm shivering, my face burns. The garage, I notice, is very gray. And brown. Brown wood walls, brown bench, gray floor, gray wires, brown and gray tools.

I don't know what to say.

"Thanks," I finally say. The look on his face when I get into my car to leave doesn't tell me anything, but I'm not really looking for anything. I just have to go.

* * *

When I get home, every thing is clear. Not ideas. I don't give a damn about ideas. I mean things. The yellow grease on the white porcelain of the stove. The chipped wood on the leg of the green armchair in the living room. Oranges stamped with red ink that says FLORIDA stacked in a blue bowl on the kitchen table. I can't stand it. The sound of the television is unbearable. Nothing feels like what it could be.

It's Sunday morning, 5 a.m.. I call into work, telling the night supervisor that my car is dead, and I have to stay home to fix it. I regret it as soon as I hang up the phone. The whole night I tried not to think or sleep or dream. Now I have the whole day. I think about waiting fifteen minutes and calling back to say my car is okay, then I hear Dad in the bathroom getting ready to go somewhere.

While he's in the shower, I dress quietly, sneak out to my car, and wait. He walks to the car carrying what looks like a heavy trash bag, balances his thermos on top of the car, and loads the trash bag in the trunk. He sips from the thermos before he gets in, then backs slowly out of the driveway. It's still dark. It's hard to secretly follow someone in a car. I can't let him get too far away or he'll go out of sight. If I get too close, he'll see me. But I don't want to lose him.

At I-96 he turns right and heads west toward Livonia. Within ten minutes he pulls into Aunt Addy's driveway. Before he's halfway up the drive, she's out the front door on the porch. He leaves his car door ajar, the motor running, and she holds her door open for him as he hefts the bag into her house. They close the door behind them. His headlights light up brown, gray, and yellow patches of grass that poke up on Aunt Addy's lawn through last week's snow. He comes back out after only a minute carrying another thermos. I follow him for a long time from expressway to expressway until, finally, he pulls into a parking lot with a sign that says, DETROIT SALT COMPANY.

Rail tracks curve between two sets of buildings: the simple wooden shack of the mine shaft opening on the left, and on the right three connected old red brick buildings. The first building on the right is short and rectangular and attached to a taller, thinner building, which is attached to a building taller and thinner yet that looks like a brick watchtower. I park down the block at the far end of the rails as they come out toward the road. Patches of muddy ice lace the ground. He simply sits in his car, lights off. He's blowing onto the steam that rises from his thermos as he looks at the mining shack, behind which the bottom of the sky is beginning to glow pale green and pink. We are the only two cars here. He must see me.

I step out of the car and slam my door. I haven't taken ten steps before he starts his car, swerves it around, and drives to the road over the rails so he won't have to look me in the eye. For now, it's enough that he's seen me.

I have to decide what to do with the day. I get back in the car, sit with my lights off and the motor running, the heating vents blowing warm air over the steering wheel onto my hands and into my eyes. At six fifteen, I go home, take a shower, call work, and tell them I'm sorry, I'll be in after all, yes, my car is working now, sure and steady as a clock.

Hector walks past me at work. When I say, "Hey," he says hello like someone is forcing him. When I see him again at the elevator and try to just kibitz, he moves items in his wire pharmacy basket from the top rack to the bottom and back again. If the muscles in his back tell the story, they say, "I wish you'd go away," so I do.

I stay at work an hour and a half later to make up the time for being late yesterday and today. I'm changing the trash in the kitchen area near the nursing desk when I see Hector push his basket into SICU on the last round of his day. I don't know whether to look at him, pretend I don't see him, or turn and walk the other way. He lifts his right hand halfway up in a somber wave as he walks by.

Before I have a chance to do anything, I hear Lynn's voice saying, "Maintenance. I'm out of paper towels in Room 12."

She must think I'm some kind of idiot. She's been sitting at the nursing desk with Sheffield talking about a date she went on last night, the movie they saw, the forest green Saab he drove, the way his lips are too thin, his earlobes large and fleshy, the fact that if he asks her out again, she'll do him. I turn to her and say, "What's your name?" She looks at me like I'm a stuffed animal she didn't know could speak.

"What?" she says.

"Your name," I say, and I point to her ID badge. "It's Lynn, isn't it?"

She gives a curt laugh and says, "Yes?"

I unclip the ID badge from my shirt pocket and hand it up to her. "Jack Fallon," I say. "You can call me Jack." I clip my ID badge back on. "Did you say Room 12, Lynn?"

"Room 12," she says.

Sheffield leans back in her chair. Her arms are crossed over her big chest, which bobs up and down with each chuckle. I head back to my cart to get more paper towels. SICU's pharmacy basket is full, and Hector has disappeared.

* * *

By the time I get home, it's nearly dusk. The windows of the house are all fogged up. Ham, I think as I open the door. Colleen, Mary, and Aunt Addy have started without me.

"Where were you?" says Aunt Addy.

"What was in the trash bag Dad gave you this morning?" I say. She turns back to her food. I say, "I was late for work today because I followed Dad to see where he was going so early on a Sunday."

She shifts her fat ass in the chair. "It's understandable that he wants to visit someone. Sometimes he comes to see me when he can't stay here."

"Why can't he stay here?" I say. "He lives here. What was in the bag?"

"Sit down and eat your dinner, Jack. No use getting all riled up over nothing. It's only stuff he's giving to Goodwill or the St. Vincent de Paul Society," she says.

"What stuff?" says Colleen.

"He wants to clean up a little of the clutter around here, that's all."

"Why can't he do that himself?" I say.

"He brings it over to see if I can use any of it, or to see if I know anyone who could. Of course, nothing fits me."

"Ma's clothes," Mary says. Her hand is at her

throat, feeling the soft skin of her neck under an orange-and-green scarf of Ma's.

"There's no reason to get you kids involved," Aunt Addy says. "I can take care of this."

"We're his children," I say. "His family."

"I'm his sister," she says. "I've known him longer. Your father sees to it that you all get along. He does the best he can. I told him I'd come over to keep an eye on you all if he needed some time to himself. He needs time to himself." She slathers butter on a dinner roll, extending her arm and pulling back her head to see the roll more clearly. As if she's talking to the melting butter, she says, "He's the only brother I have."

When she bites into the roll, flaky brown crumbs fall in an avalanche over the sloping mounds of her body that push out against her dark blue sweater. She relaxes her arm into an *L*, the half-eaten roll pinched between her middle finger and her thumb, and she swallows. "It's a very sad thing that happened to your mother. You may not want to hear it, but her drinking drove a wedge between them. You know, you're very lucky nobody else was hurt in that accident."

I want to choke her. Instead, I shake my head back and forth, back and forth.

Mary's hand is on my arm. "Jack," she's saying. "Jack. Stop it. Jack. You're scaring me."

"Jack," says Colleen, and she takes my other arm. I shake away.

"Alone" is the only word I can say.

Then I leave.

I left without my coat, and the car is cold. I start the car, turn off the heat, and roll down the windows. I need to feel the cold on my skin. I used to love these steel gray winter days where it seemed nothing would ever happen: days when the world, stuck in its own frozen beauty, tilts toward dusk, everything still except the flash under the streetlights of silver dots of snow flying in all the wrong directions.

Driving east down I-96, I see cars: sheet metal, glass, and steel careen over concrete at over seventy miles an hour.

By the time I get to Hector's, I'm nearly frozen. I turn off the car and sit in front of his house for about fifteen minutes before I decide. I can't even feel my knuckles when I knock on the door.

"Do you want to go for a drive?" I ask him. He's looking at me like I'm crazy, so I say it again. "Do you want to go for a drive? You said you'd show me around downtown by the University. Maybe we could do that now."

"Okay," he says, "wait a minute." He comes out with his coat and another coat for me, but I shake my head no. In the car he's only talking directions. "At the end of Honora, turn right, then left right away at the first light." Hector turns the heat on high and I roll up the window. "Once we get onto the expressway," he continues, "the exchanges and exits come quickly, so pay attention."

Did you like it when you kissed me? I could ask him. *Would you like to do it again?* I may not like what he says.

"Cross the overpass and make another left onto the freeway," Hector says.

The Ambassador Bridge looms to our right over the Detroit River. Windsor blinks in the distance.

I could ask Dad, *Do you remember the first time Ma kissed you? Do you ever think about it?* The more I drive, the more questions I have.

"Once you get onto I-75, follow the Rosa Parks/ Civic Center sign. It's just up ahead on the right."

The brake lights of cars ahead of me glow red, then dim. The white lights from oncoming traffic on the other side of the median flash by.

Hector says, "Take Civic Center on the left to the Lodge going north, then from the right-hand lane, look for the Warren exit just past the Canfield overpass."

The air from the heater and my turn signal are the only other sounds between us. The car's warming up.

The blood is coming back into my fingers, my toes, my ears, every part of me that was frozen, and it's beginning to hurt.

A Little Give-and-Take

Of course, Dad was pissed when the police called. I suppose he was more scared than pissed at first, because the last time they called, it was about the crash that killed Ma. So when they only told him I'd been caught shoplifting, yeah, I guess that was when he got pissed. I wish he were one of those men who yelled and screamed or threw things when he was mad. Instead, he wore his anger as a disappointment on his face that just kills a person to look at. I felt afraid and sorry for him at the same time, ashamed to have put him through feeling this way again.

And the whole scene at the store was all so needlessly dramatic. They handcuffed me and everything, drove me to the station as if I were a real criminal. They let me go on my own recognizance because it was my first offense, but Dad had to come pick me up, then drive me back to the lot at Bavarian Village to get my car. Jesus. Twenty years old, and I had to have my father pick me up from the police station. I would've called Jack or Mary, but I didn't know their work numbers by heart.

"A salami, Colleen?" Dad said on the drive back to Bavarian Village. "You tried to steal salami?"

I hadn't done it for any *reason* or anything, so it was impossible to explain. On the plus side, it gave us something to talk about. On the minus side, I had nothing to say. We listened to the radio announcer talk about the election, opining what President Carter would do in his last months before Reagan took over. The gray-and-beige one-story storefronts on Fenkell flit by in silence. Rows of auto repair shops, tool and die makers, window glass repair shops, oil change centers, and car washes were broken up now and again with a fast food restaurant, a Dairy Queen, a church.

"It wasn't salami," I finally said. "It was chorizo. I thought we could use it for the stuffing on Thanksgiving." I pronounced *chorizo* the way my high school Spanish teacher told me the Spaniards say it, with a *th* instead of a *z* sound, so Dad would know I wasn't a complete idiot.

The next night Aunt Addy was in the kitchen again, plopped in her spot waiting to be fed and giving advice as if she were doing us some big damned favor. But she didn't say a word about the shoplifting. She saves things like that for special occasions to hit you with when you're low so she can really grind it in, or when you're up so she can knock you down. "I just came by to say hello," she said, by which she means to eat, and be nosey, and babysit grown adults while Dad is off doing whatever he does when he's not home. Had Dad's avoiding us been something serious, Addy would have never been able to keep her trap shut about it. Something big and dramatic like prostitutes, or drugs, or gambling, or bank robbery would be easier to explain, though, in my book. If it was just that he didn't want to be around us anymore since Ma died, that's a little harder to swallow, as if he suddenly realized he didn't love us after all.

Addy's been coming over three times a week since before I can remember, but Dad and Ma were always here to listen to her blather. With Ma dead and Dad avoiding us, it's just weird having her around eating, looking, nudging.

"You kids never go to Mass since your mother died," she said. "Didn't she bring you up better than this?"

Mary stood up, saying, "I have a date."

Aunt Addy's eyes followed Mary walking away, but her head never moved. Her attention shifted to Jack and her hands started. "Your hair is so thick!" She squirmed her pale, wormy fingers through his soft dark curls and said, "You'll make some woman very happy one of these days. A real lady-killer you're going to be." Jack smiled, but didn't move until she took her hand back. He finished eating, placed his fork, his knife, his spoon one by one on his plate, carried it all to the sink, and washed them.

I touched the rim of the platter with one finger when Addy reached for another piece of meatloaf. "Why don't we save that for Dad?" I said. "Ma always liked to leave him a little gift in the refrigerator when he came home late."

"Your father works so hard, Colleen." She pressed her back against the Naugahyde until the chair's casters squealed. "I'm the same way. Your grandpa used to say, 'If you have time to play, then you're not working hard enough!'"

"Dad's not at work, Aunt Addy. Nobody works that much."

She helped herself to more potatoes, forked them into her mouth, and swallowed so quickly, she couldn't possibly have had time to taste. I made a plate for Dad, covered it with aluminum foil to protect it from Addy if she were to look in the fridge later.

"You should probably get home now," I said. "Don't worry about us, Aunt Addy. We can take care of ourselves. We're all adults."

Some people are givers and some are takers. Givers put something back into the world. Ma increased her world with music and cooking, and people gravitated around her. I have her brown eyes and auburn hair. Her pure, generous love made us feel alive, important, whole. Since she's gone, our tight-knit family is unraveling. Dad has his books and goes missing most of our days. When Jack isn't working, he's sleeping. Mary's gone every night, off with some new guy or other, or going to dance bars with her punk rock friends. I come home to cook after work, but besides me, Addy's the only one ever here at home, and she doesn't even live here. She sits and gobbles up the world—our food, everybody's business, Dad's attention. The only thing she puts back into the world is her negative attitude. Her focus is always on what we lack.

When Ma was alive, Dad's love for us was apparent, but now he's like a fan stuck in the off position, neither sucking the life out of the world, nor blowing life and love back into the room. He could go either way, and it scares me.

The other night when I got home from the bank, Dad and Addy sat in the kitchen talking. I was hanging up my coat in the closet trying to listen when, just before Dad got up with another book and left, I was sure I heard her say, "She wants attention," which is ridiculous. I never wanted to get caught shoplifting, so in fact I wanted as little attention as possible. It was the things I took that demanded attention; something about the shape or color would announce itself and I'd think, *That's for me.*

My favorite canvas bag, sky blue with a big green-and-yellow daisy embroidered on both sides, was the first thing I took. I saw it in Hudson's and spent some time unfolding and folding it. I set it back on the shelf, walked around other departments, then came back to fold and unfold it again. And then it was mine. Nothing after that was as satisfying. I'd get home and unload pens, watches, sandals, etc., onto the bed, but under my bedroom light, it all just looked like a bunch of junk. I ended up giving away most of it as nicely wrapped anonymous gifts for the other girls at work. It caused quite a stir for a while. There are only ten of us, so I had to give myself a cute little Spanish fan made of black lace so nobody would guess I was the person bestowing gifts. But I stopped wasting gifts on that lot when I heard Virginia, a sad, skinny woman with five parakeets, complain about the yarn I'd discreetly left for her. I'd never even seen the woman smile before, and suddenly she laughs this nasty laugh and says, "What the hell am I supposed to do with *one* skein of yarn? It's not even enough to knit a small scarf." It started a chain reaction of mockery. Had the women at work known the gifts were from me, I'm sure they'd have appreciated them more.

But store-gotten gifts are cheap and stupid anyway. The only real gift I have for the world is my voice. Cooking is a labor of love, but singing comes as naturally as breathing for me. Two days after the chorizo incident, I saw the SINGER WANTED ad in the *Metro Times*, and it made me feel the way coming home used to feel: safe, right, absolutely happy. I pictured the whole family together at a table in a club listening to me sing, and even though Ma wouldn't be there, the love she gave us would manifest in the music. I thought this could be the answer to everything. Auditions were being held the day before Thanksgiving at a place downtown near Wayne State. The guy on the phone told me when to show up and said, "Bring your own music."

When I was younger, when Mary had gone off to Sister Immaculata in first grade and Jack was still a baby, Dad worked the afternoon shift as an electrician at historical Greenfield Village and Henry Ford Museum. Mornings, I would sit at the kitchen table and ask him to play coffee. Ma didn't bump her way along the walls from the bedroom to the kitchen until around eleven o'clock every day. He'd measure the coffee, set the fire burning under the tin percolator, then get my favorite glass mug, frosted powder blue on the outside, white on the inside. The inch of brown coffee at the bottom of the cup would lighten with milk as Dad poured, then added three teaspoons of sugar. When the toast came up, I'd say *Pop!* and he'd soften the blackened toast with butter, and sprinkle brown sugar all over it. I colored Snoopy blue and orange, every once in a while looking up to watch Dad's fine-point pen mark its way across the crossword puzzle page.

He's on the day shift now, and a few months after Ma's accident, I started getting up early in the morning to reestablish the coffee tradition with Dad. I figured after we got comfortable with each other again, he might start to talk. We sat for the first part of the week sipping coffee in happy silence. Then one morning I tried to make small talk, but he brushed my questions aside with one-word answers until, exasperated, I spit out, "Dad, we never talk anymore."

He looked at me hard for the first time in a long time, like I was his little girl and he was worried about me. He sipped his coffee slowly, set it down, and said, "What is there to say?" He brushed the table with the back of his hand as if there were crumbs, and looked at me again. "I know people talk all the time," he continued. "I listen to them at work. Sometimes I go to movies by myself and listen as I wait for the reel to begin. And I think: *Really? That's so important that you have to say it out loud to another person?* Weather, news, politics. Turn on the TV or read the paper and it's the same thing. Or shopping. People spend a lot of time talking about *sales*. Curtains. Shoes. Cucumbers. When was the last time you had anything really worth talking about?"

"When Ma died."

"Right. And talking about it won't change anything."

"Still, a conversation with a little give-and-take never hurt anyone."

He shook his head slowly.

"So we're just supposed to never talk now? That won't make anyone happy."

"It hasn't even been a year yet, Colleen. Give it a little while. Try to make fake happy, and it all turns to shit." He chuckled a little, which was good to see. He looked at his watch, said, "Time for work." I turned to go take my morning shower.

"Coll?" he said. I turned back. "Try to be nicer to Addy, okay?"

It wasn't much, but it was a start. I figured every day it would get a little easier, but the next morning he walked into the kitchen shortly after I'd ground enough beans for a full pot. He shoved another book into his jacket pocket, and said, "Only make enough for yourself. I'll stop at Dunkin' Donuts." He quickly turned up the corners of his mouth to simulate a smile, and left.

The coffee machine hissed, groaned, and started to drip. I reached up on top of the fridge to retrieve the seam ripper from the sewing box stashed there and continued upstairs to Dad's bedroom. This time, underwear, middle drawer on the left. At the crotch of his boxer shorts there's a button of material where all the fabric comes together. The threads separated nicely under the slightest movement of the sharp hook. I was careful not to open too much, just enough to afford a strange breeze as he walked through his day: a little ghost of air. Pulling the tiny threads makes it look like natural wear and tear, or a manufacturer's defect. I made a sliver of a hole in the back seam of one more pair of underwear, undid four or five stitches from the underarm of a dress shirt, loosened one thread of a button on another shirt so it would eventually fall off on its own, then slipped downstairs before Mary and Jack got up and ready for school and work.

I cupped my hands around the powder blue mug to get warm. I burned the toast, smothered it with butter and brown sugar, and ate breakfast. With a lot of concentration and a little luck, everything was okay for a moment or two. The coffee was perfect.

There are more than a few pictures I can't get out of my head: the look of Ma's hair pulled up and back on her head when it was hot, or when she cooked; the way the hair blanketed one shoulder when she played the guitar.

"Move a little bit when you sing," she'd say. "Don't just stand there like a lump."

When I asked: *How?* she said: *Listen*. She sat on the cherrywood piano bench in the living room to play the guitar, a reprint of *The Last Supper* hanging behind her head, raised both hands to pull the hair back from her face while she thought of something to play. The tanned leather of the guitar strap that fell heavily over one breast made her look like a saint on a Mass card: the patron saint of music, or of hair.

"You've got a voice like honey," she said. "I have a voice like wet garbage. If I had a voice like you . . ." She looked down at her guitar and cocked her ear to tune it, stretching one string, plucking another, twisting the tuning pegs. She looked up when she finished. "But you're full-bodied, nice hips, big boobs. Don't blush, it's just a fact. Mary and Jack are lanky like your father. Use everything you've got, not just your voice."

Then she shook her hair, moved her hands into place, the pads of her fingers touched the strings, her hands fluttered like a bird taking off, and I could almost taste it: a salsa version with a slower tempo. I took a breath, and in a low deep voice I slowly began "In the Still of the Night." My arms and torso and legs and feet followed the words and the strings, and

I felt it, body moving with voice, arms bending on the trill of low note, hips shifting to shimmy, and when I was dancing and singing for the old people in the nursing home with Ma strumming along, my tight new teenage body swaying and bending, the whole routine came together, and I became a star. The people sat in their wheelchairs and in lounge chairs covered in orange and teal plastic, their gray-yellow skin slack over the bones of their faces, their eyes round and dry but focused on me. They were happy. They swayed and sometimes they cried as they listened, but when they thanked me later, touched my face with a shaky hand sprouting chipped, yellow fingernails, when they said hello, I was happy to be mistaken for someone named Miriam or Ida, someone they thought they knew giving them joy, and when I left, I knew: This is my gift. I can make people happy for a little while, a small spark of a moment to light their way when they need it, flash, and who knows how long before it's gone, but when it comes, it's brilliant, and it's true.

Some people are addicted to unhappiness, and Aunt Addy is one of them. She had come over once again when nobody else was home to sit sentry on me. It was just the two of us, so I had to try to be civil.

"You'll be here for Thanksgiving?" I asked.

She heaved a heavy sigh. "Yes," she said, "Doris—

Dr. Harrington's nurse at work? Begged me to spend the day with her husband and their kids." She shook her head. "Those kids love me. Climb all over me. They're wonderful, but it's exhausting."

With elbows on the table, her eyes shifted back and forth, followed me around the kitchen. I washed the empty pop bottles to take back to the store.

"Besides," she says, "this is the first Thanksgiving since your mother died. Poor Hannah."

The pop bottles glugged out suds.

"The AMA just released a report that says people who spend holidays with family are healthier than those who spend them apart," she said. "People separated from their families by long distances have many more maladies and afflictions. It's a medical fact."

Aunt Addy takes more than ten pills a day for diabetes, high blood pressure, aches and pains in her legs because of the extra weight. She leaned forward and said: "Would you be a doll and put the kettle on?"

"Sure. What kind of tea do you want?"

"Green, thanks." She moved her huge black purse off the chair next to her and lifted one leg, resting it where the purse sat. Her breath heaved hard.

"Your father and I have spent every Thanksgiving together since the day he was born. Except for those first few years after they got married."

"Shit. We're out of green. All we have is oolong."

"Oo-who?" Her voice was high and crackly.

"It's Chinese, I think. Black, not green."

She dug into her purse for something, arm buried up to the elbow. "Oh, all right," she said. "That'll be fine, I guess." She squinched one eye and curled up the corner of her mouth, leaning into her purse. When she found what she was looking for, her face relaxed. We waited for the kettle to rumble and hiss.

"Nobody should ever have to spend Thanksgiving all alone," she said. With a paperclip, she chipped flecks of red polish off her fingernails. Most of the flakes skittered across the kitchen table; some fell on the floor.

The Tuesday before Thanksgiving, I walked in the front door to see Dad unpacking groceries from brown paper bags on the kitchen table. A frozen Butterball turkey, cranberry sauce, cranberry jelly, the store-bought stuffing I would never in a million years use, eight different kinds of vegetables frozen and canned, a ten-pound bag of potatoes, onions, tomatoes, celery, cream cheese, Mrs. Paul's Onion Soup Mix, real butter, and six bottles of red wine. I hadn't seen so much wine since before Ma died, since I realized that the wine was more than just a tingle on her tongue, the rush of blood through her cheeks. I shook the hair out of my eyes. Dad glanced quickly from my hair to my eyes, then his attention suddenly shifted to the floor, then the turkey, as if he'd been caught doing something he shouldn't have.

Jack ambled into the kitchen after his nap asking, "What's all this stuff?" A yellow sleepy sat on the end of one of his eyelashes. Dad put his right hand at the back of Jack's head and applied his left thumb to Jack's eye. He swept away the sleepy, then stood back.

Dad said, "We have to have turkey on Thanksgiving, right?"

I didn't say anything about the turkey in the freezer I'd gotten just before they banned me forever from Bavarian Village. I was happy to see that he was trying.

"I'm working Thursday," Jack said. "I get paid time plus time-and-a-half."

"When do you get home?" Dad asked.

"Four o'clock."

"Time enough." Dad clapped Jack on the shoulder, squeezed, let go. "Dinner doesn't start until six. Although I told people they could start coming over around four or five, so you'll be just in time for everything." Dad folded the bags, set one on top of the other using a canned ham to press them all down.

"People?" I said.

Mary walked in and put her books on the table

next to the ham with all the bags underneath it. "What's all this?" she said. Dad stood between the table and the trash compactor. Jack leaned against the refrigerator door, his hospital ID badge still hanging from a pocket of his navy blue maintenance uniform. I was in the middle of the room, freestanding with nothing to lean against, so I walked quickly to the bedroom to change out of my work clothes.

When I came back, I said, "Dad, I was planning for just us."

"We'll have plenty of food, Colleen," he said. "You won't have to do a thing."

"I want to help."

"No," he insisted. "Addy and I have it covered. Invite some friends if you want. Just let us know how many so we have enough food." He carried his shoes from the foyer into the kitchen to put them on. Two toes poked out of his sock.

"Dad, look at you. Put on another pair. I'll fix those for you."

"No, no. It's just a pair of socks. Easy enough to replace."

"No, really."

"No," he said. "Really." Any simulation of patience or enjoyment at being home left his voice. He bunched up the material at the end of the sock with his forefinger, twisted it, and shoved the knot between two toes to close the hole before he slipped his foot into the shoe. Then he left again to get something he said he forgot from the store.

The singing auditions were held in a loft downtown in the warehouse district with a view of the Ambassador Bridge through the floor-to-ceiling windows. The wood floors were splintered, and they warped so that you limped when you walked the length of the room. A long shelf filled with crazy-looking Kewpie dolls lined one wall. Other than that, the only other furniture in the room was a mic stand near the piano and three folding chairs, where a girl my age with hair ratted about a foot high sat next to a tremendously ugly man. His carbuncular nose was the texture of pitted cement. A fat older lady sat at the piano.

I'd gained a little weight and gone up two sizes since Ma died, but even my new clothes were beginning to bind. I was sure I'd lose the weight again once everything got back to normal, but in the meantime, I'd bought a dress one more size up for the audition. I figured if I wore something that was a little loose, I'd look thinner, like a proper chanteuse. I took my daisy bag for good luck, but the ugly man pointed to me as soon as I walked in and barked, "Get your music. Put your bags under the shelves there, and stand in line there." He seemed irritated at me from the start, as if

I were some sort of idiot for not knowing the layout and procedure of the audition.

About twenty singers preceded me, but none were any good, and the three judges told them so in no uncertain terms, so I was feeling confident by the time they got to me." Colleen Fallon," the girl with the ratted hair said. "What's that, Jewish?"

I laughed, but she didn't, and I realized she wasn't kidding. "It's Irish," I said.

"Okay, we're wasting time," said the ugly man. He snapped his fingers, pointed from my head to my feet, and said, "Come on. Let's hear what you got."

I handed the fat lady my music. I'd brought "Lover Man (Oh, Where Can You Be?)," "Blue Gardenia," "Good Morning Heartache," and "I Gotta Right to Sing the Blues," among others.

"Oh," the fat lady said. She looked at the ugly man as if asking for help. Then she shrugged. "Okay, 'Cry Me a River,' then."

Unlike any of the other people, they let me sing the whole song, which I thought was a good sign. When I'd finished, the girl said, "Do you have anything else?"

I motioned to the piano player, who shook her head.

"No," the girl said, "I mean something modern. We're looking for something a bit more . . . now, you know? Torch songs aren't really cool at the moment." The ugly man grunted, and the girl continued, "We'll have a whole band; guitars and drums and such." She held up drumsticks.

"We're looking for something rock, or punk, or something," the ugly man said. "Nobody listens to those songs anymore. Know that song, 'Because the Night'?"

I shook my head no. "What about 'People'?" I said, but they all looked at me with blank faces. I'd learned it for one of our trips to the nursing home with Ma. Jack helped me memorize it, and even sang along when I was practicing it in the living room, with him mimicking Barbra by crossing his eyes, and moving his hands and mouth the way she does. I never saw Dad laugh so hard in my life.

To wipe the blank off their faces, I said, "'People.' You know, the Barbra Streisand one? I don't have the music, but I can do it without." I started, "People . . ." but everybody—the fat lady, the ratty-haired girl, the ugly man, and all the people in line behind me—started laughing in a big obnoxious chorus of laughs.

The ugly man put up his hand either to stop me, or to settle himself from what looked like the pain of laughing so hard. The fat lady said, "You sing well, but your music isn't interesting. If this is all you can do . . ." I nodded, and the three of them chuckled themselves slowly to a stop. The ugly man shook his head and called the next person. The next singer squawked and the man swore, while I gathered my bag. The Kewpie dolls were ugly and nothing I would ever want, but I took four of them anyway.

Luckily, I hadn't told anyone about the audition, so I didn't have to look like a failure. I threw the dolls one by one out the window on the expressway as I drove home.

When I got home, I plopped down on the bed to watch Mary get ready for a date. "Who are these people he's bringing to our Thanksgiving?" I asked her.

"Dunno. Probably people from work." She turned left and right to watch herself in the full-length mirror hanging on the closet door.

"Do you think it's a woman?"

"I don't know, Coll," she said in a protracted sigh. "I haven't met them either, have I?"

"Why's he bringing strange people here anyway?"

"When we have so many strange people here already," Mary said.

She slipped on a faded black top that fit her thin body snugly. It had a little V-neck that showed off the black bead hanging from a thin silver chain around her neck. She ran her hands over the soft cotton of the top, tilted her hips back and forth to show off the short purple skirt that looked like it was made of quilted silk sewn with some sort of Chinese pattern in the threading. Still looking in the mirror, she asked, "Trying too hard?"

"It looks sort of weird."

"Weird?" She hopped up and down in a thrashing dance to the music she had playing on the stereo. The music crushed and bumped into itself while some singer shouted something with the word "anarchy" in it.

"I've never seen a skirt like that."

"That's the point. Right? Who wants to wear something anyone else could wear?"

My half of the closet held three different colors of the same plain skirt I wore to work with one of five identical white blouses. Both sets of the smaller sizes I wore the year before sat bunched in a garbage bag at the back of the closet until I can fit into them again. I said, "Ask Jack, then."

Mary pranced into the living room, where Jack lay on the floor playing solitaire. I turned off the stereo to look for something more melodic among her records.

In the silence, I heard Jack say, "Frit Froo," in imitation of a whistle.

"Too much?" Mary asked.

"Where you going?"

"Movies."

"I like," he said, keeping the word *like* in his mouth for an extra-long time.

Mary giggled.

"A lot," he said. "What shoes you wearing?"

Mary and Jack came back into the room. I picked an album with a black cover with white lines crawling back and forth on it.

Jack saw me and took the record. "You wouldn't like it."

"But . . ." I pointed to the word *Joy* in the band's name on the cover.

He filed the album back in the milk crate Mary kept next to her bookshelf. Mary put a different shoe on each foot, one lime green Chuck Taylor sneaker, one black army boot. Jack leaned against the doorjam, holding out a hand, squinched one eye, then moved his hand to consider the other shoe.

"Are you bringing anyone to Thanksgiving?" I asked Jack.

"Who would I bring?" he said, slightly annoyed. "Boot, I think," he told Mary. "Too cold for sneakers."

"Some of the guys from the swim team maybe."

"I left in the middle of the season. We don't . . . I don't really keep in touch."

"Visible sock? No?" Mary asked.

"Slightly visible sock. White." He turned to me. "Why? Are you bringing someone?"

I folded my arms across my chest and gave him the stare.

"Well, I don't know," he said, and laughed.

Mary kicked off the sneaker and the boot and put on two other kinds of shoe. Jack grabbed the pile of cast-off clothes from the chair in the corner and held them in both hands, gesturing toward the floor. "May I?" he said. He bent his waist in a bow.

"Go ahead. They're all Mary's anyway."

He chucked them to the floor and sat in the chair. He pointed to Mary's left foot. Mary kicked off both shoes. She pulled on white socks and laced up the army boots.

Jack said, "So, Dad's the only one bringing anybody?"

"Yep," I said. "Do you know who these people are?"

"Nope." He clicked his teeth twice to show his final approval of Mary's outfit. "Welp"—he stood up—"we'll find out tomorrow, huh?"

"That we will," said Mary. "What about the cleavage?" she asked me.

"Not too much. Just enough." I laughed and added, "Did you do the M&M test?"

Mary laughed and Jack asked, "What's the M&M test?"

"In junior high, when we all first started wearing bras, we decided the best way to figure out if your boobs were too smooshed together is if you drop an M&M down the bra. If it drops out, you're okay."

Jack's face lit up. "Plain or peanut?"

"Well . . ." Mary laughed.

"Depends who you ask . . ." I pointed to Mary's perky pair of pears, she to my melons.

"Anyway," I said, "you look good. As usual."

She took one last look in the mirror and left behind a pile of shoes lying scattered over the floor, some singly, some in pairs. I considered them for a moment, but decided not to try them on later. I would never wear any of them, even if they did fit.

Jack stood up to go, but I blocked his way.

"I need you to help me find a song to sing. Something modern."

"Why?"

"Just because, okay?"

"Geez. Okay. Like what, though?"

"Like the stuff you and Mary listen to. Not that anarchy stuff, though."

Jack looked at me with his patient wise-man-on-a-mountaintop look. He sat and thought, looking at me the whole time, then slowly hoisted himself up to riffle through Mary's milk crate of albums. He pulled out a record with four men dressed in deep-sea diving gear and showed it to me as if I'd know anything about them. I shrugged.

"No," he said, and refiled the record. He riffled, paused, riffled, and paused again to look back up at me. Finally, he pulled out an album and unfolded it to show me the full picture of three half-clad women holding spears. I squinched my face in doubt, but he handed me the sleeve as he set the record on the stereo.

"Lemme try a few first. Be honest, though. If you really don't like it, you shouldn't do it."

"I could probably, though."

He shook his head. "Never pretend to like something if you really don't. It's just not cool."

"Pffft," I said. "Cool. What's cool got to do with it?"

"Cool is knowing what you really like even if nobody else does." He started the turntable spinning, placed the needle gently on the first song, but let it play for only a few seconds.

"That sounds nice."

He shook his head, and continued with the same routine through three more songs. On the fifth, he stood back, pointed to the lyrics on the cover.

"'My Only Love,'" he said.

"I like the music." When the man started singing, I said, "I like his voice."

"Yes," Jack said.

I read along as the man sang. When it had finished, Jack lifted the needle and set it back.

"I love it," I said.

"I thought you might."

"How? How did you know?"

Sometimes when Jack smiled, his face took on the best of Mom and Dad, and looking at him sitting there all quiet and relaxed, it felt like we were all one again. "I know you," he said, and for a second this embarrassed me because I know he knew the good in me and the bad in me too.

"Do you think other people will like it?" I asked.

"Other people who? You like it. I like it. Other people don't matter. You know how to make a song your own. Hang on."

He ran out of the room, and in a few minutes came back with Ma's guitar. He set the record spinning again, placed the needle, and propped the record sleeve with the lyrics on his knee to read along while the song played. When it had finished, he turned off the stereo, shifted his gaze between the lyrics and the floor, then began to pick and strum experimentally on the guitar. I hadn't seen him play since Ma died. As he picked out a tune to match the song on the stereo, it felt like we were all coming back to life, that there was a possibility we could become normal again. Even though it was only Ma's guitar that was still here and not Ma herself, it was something we could make a new life with. With her guitar in his hands, Jack transformed back into his old self: happy, fun, interested. If we could do this more often, him arranging a tune with me singing along, everything would be okay. Dad would see that we could be a family again, all together with each other, and that this was the best way to keep Ma alive in our hearts.

After a few minutes of fiddling around on the guitar, he said, "It's so sad," with a laugh, and then set the guitar aside. "It shouldn't be too hard to make your own arrangement." And then, as suddenly and completely as he'd come alive, he deflated again. He rubbed both hands over his face, and said, "I better get to bed."

"You'll help me with the arrangement?"

He shook his head. "Best you do it. I'll listen, though," he said sadly, then forced a little smile. "It'll be good."

He turned to go. I almost stopped him, but didn't. I wanted to thank him, I wanted to hug him, but it felt too hokey, and anyway I figured he knew what was what.

Thanksgiving morning, Mary and I played casino in the den, both of us sitting on the floor, using the ottoman as a table for the cards. The Thanksgiving Day Parade was on television, while pans rattled and pots clanked in the kitchen. Mary had never had any musical talent, so I thought maybe she'd understand about the audition, but I still wasn't sure I wanted to tell anyone.

"Stop humming," Mary said.

"I'm not humming."

"Or at least if you're going to hum, then hum a real song. You sound like Mrs. Nash from the nursing home."

"Stop."

"It's true. Do you remember? She'd rock back and forth no matter what Ma played, and groan one long groan, louder and louder the more she got excited. They had to put a bib around her tiny neck every time you sang."

"Oh God."

"That's quite a compliment, I'd say." Mary shuffled the deck and let me cut. "Poor thing," she said, "just one long grunt."

"Kind of like when you sing," I said, even though I knew it was mean.

"Kinda," said Mary.

Aunt Addy poked her head through the door.

"How you girls doing?" She bent with a rasping sigh to kiss her wet sloppy kiss on Mary's cheek, then on mine.

"Hi, Aunt Addy," Mary said. "Need some help out there?"

"Nope. We're doing just dandy. You girls sit tight. Look." She kept her left hand behind her back, and with her right hand set down a miniature turkey and a miniature Indian with a colorful, elaborate headdress. "The judges at the Miniature Makers Confab told me I needed to try my hand at animals and people. They said it might increase my chances of placing higher next year at the competition."

"Cute," Mary said.

"Cute isn't the point," said Addy. "It's art."

"Oh," I said. "*Art.*"

She straightened her back and smiled. "I also brought you some of my famous cookies." The hand behind her back suddenly revealed a red tin brimming with green waxed paper. M&M's peaked out of the browned fork rows in the peanut butter cookies. Mary and I each took one and praised the cookies and her generosity.

"I thought you'd like that," Aunt Addy said. "It's not often you get a real treat, huh?" She stroked my hair as if I were a pet. "I guess I'll get back to the kitchen to help your father with the stuffing."

"I can help," I said.

"No, dear. No. Of course, it won't have any of that fancy salami you seem to like so much, or anything like that. Just good, simple stuffing. Pour it from the box and add butter." She balanced the tin in her hand, and we all watched the parade. Bullwinkle listed and swayed down Woodward Avenue. "They ought to be careful," she said before she clumped back to the kitchen. "A couple of years ago the Pink Panther hit a light post, blew apart, and killed someone's grandmother."

The parade was ending. Santa stood on a building high above the crowd in downtown Detroit waving, stroking his beard, patting his belly. This was the big moment, the one everyone waited for. His microphone wasn't working properly—some words came through, while others drifted off back to the North Pole. "Joy," he shouted. "Happy," we heard through the screaming feedback. He stood on top of a roof shooting these words down at the crowd below and at all the people watching at home. He was waving like a madman.

Jack came home from work at four o'clock sharp. Instead of taking his usual nap, he showered and came out in a white button-down shirt, tapered straight leg jeans, and new black loafers with white socks. Jack's skin was smooth and clear and very pale, which made his brown eyes look almost as black as his hair. He looked different out of his maintenance uniform. He was thin as a knotted rope pulled tight, lanky with a little bit of muscle. Mary, hair in a carefully disarranged bouffant-like upsweep, twirled a few strands of fallen hair at her temple around her finger as she talked to Jack at the table. She wanted to know what was the goriest thing he'd seen while cleaning at the hospital. He wouldn't say.

"But I like it there," he said. "I feel invisible. I can walk into a nursing station and nobody even looks up. I hear everything."

"Doesn't that bug you?" Mary wanted to know.

Dad had about four projects going at once. He basted the turkey, mixed onion soup mix with the cream cheese to make stuffed celery, checked the potatoes to see if they were boiled enough to start mashing. When I walked over to look at the turkey, he said, "I've got it. You go sit down."

"It's like being a ghost," Jack said. "As long as I keep busy, nobody notices me. It's only when I stand still that I suddenly appear to them. Then they reach for their purses and lower their voices. All I have to do is get busy and they forget me again."

He got up for a glass of milk. Aunt Addy rearranged the waxed paper in the half-empty tin.

"Don't ruin your dinner by stuffing yourself with these cookies," she told Jack before he'd even taken one.

I wore black slacks with one of my white work blouses. Mary had changed into a canary yellow vintage cocktail dress with purple pointy-toed, short-heeled pumps. I thought she looked silly with her Breakfast at Tiffany's bouffant, but had it still been the sixties, I suppose she would've been considered elegant.

When he came back to the table, Mary said, "You look so cute, Jack." She pinched the butt of his jeans and pulled him closer. "Nice belt." She poked a finger underneath the belt to get a closer look. Jack blushed and pulled away.

The clack and swoosh of the front door brought in the first batch of guests, and others followed shortly after. I'd thought there would be only two or three other people, but seven or eight of Dad's work friends showed up, none of whom I knew except for Smitty, Dad's old friend who smelled like cigarettes and peppermint. Each time a new person entered, the crisp cold air rushed into the house, and the turkey smell grew more tantalizing. Someone carried a Tupperware dish with something green and brown inside. Someone else offered a bag of donuts for dessert. Dinner was clacking plates, laughing, and about ten conversations going at once.

Dad lifted a spoonful of green Jell-O dotted with brown to his lips and asked the woman who brought it: "Are these raisins in here, Char?" She had short mousy hair spiked like needles coming out of her head, and large hands with fingernails gnawed so closely that the ends of her fingers looked like loaves of uncooked dough left to rise.

"Nope," she told him. "Bacon bits."

"Mmm," Dad said. "Jack?"

With a large spoon, Jack scooped a dollop of Jell-O onto his plate and passed it down, the bacon gleaming brown through the clear green of the Jell-O. Aunt Addy was the only one to decline. "No thank you," she said to Mary. Then in a loud whisper to Char: "It's just that bacon gives me gas."

A bald man with crooked teeth named Stosh said, "Here's my Thanksgiving toast: Thank God we have a new president. Maybe Reagan'll have the balls to get the hostages away from those towelheads." During the hot silence that followed, Addy tried to finish crunching a piece of stuffed celery so she could say something, but Smitty jumped in to cut the tension with a story about another electrician at work who let his dog run around the historic grounds of Greenfield Village until it developed a lewd fondness for the leg of one of the candle makers. The candle maker and the other electrician laughed extra loud for a long time. I sat back for a second and looked around. Everyone seemed happy.

There was a small glimmer of butter in the corner of Dad's mouth. The turkey tasted so good, I thought I might cry. It was as moist as a ripe peach.

To be polite, I'd taken a little Jell-O for myself, thinking it might be possible to put it in my mouth and swallow without chewing or tasting it. When I rested a chunk of it on my tongue, the lime flavor was both tangy and sweet. Right before I swallowed, the cured salty taste of the bacon came through, complementing perfectly the tangy sweetness. Astonishing. I would have never dreamed it could be that good.

Three beer cans sat on top of the piano on cork coasters with pictures of a red harp. Dad sat on the piano bench shifting back and forth talking to Smitty and a few of the others, who sat on the couch or on fold-out card table chairs. I sat on one arm of the couch, Addy had the green armchair, Jack and Mary were on the floor with their backs against the wall.

I stood up and said, "Give us a tune, Dad."

Addy sat forward. "Do, James. Please. You and Colleen sing so lovely together."

"No," he said, "I think my voice is giving out with old age."

"Oh pooh," Aunt Addy said.

"I'll sing to you," I said. "How's that?"

I felt the shaking in my stomach, the stir of heat that drives a song. My throat was moist and my lungs full. When my chest expanded, there was a feeling less than an itch, more than a tingle, ready for a song. At least here, I knew my gift was appreciated.

"Get up. Let me look for something to play." I gave him a gentle push, my hand on his shoulder. His torso bent slightly, but he stayed sitting.

Aunt Addy quickly brought her hands together, making one loud clap.

"No," he insisted. "We've got company. That's enough entertainment. Right?" He raised his beer to Smitty's, and clinked. A few others lifted their drinks in the air before taking deep swigs.

"I don't mind," I said.

"James," said Aunt Addy. "She wants to sing."

Jack's head rested on Mary's shoulder.

"I'll play for you," Aunt Addy said. She shifted her body forward in the chair, strained to stand up.

"No thanks!" Dad said, laughing. He waved his hand at the end of his outstretched arm. "You're not exactly known for your virtuoso performances, Adelaide."

Aunt Addy's lips slowly flattened out against her teeth in a smile that looked like she was checking her teeth in the mirror for lipstick.

"No," she said. She settled back into the chair. "No. I guess you're the musical part of the family. You and Colleen and Jack." She folded the napkin that held her cookie into a tiny white triangle. "And of course, Hannah, when she was alive. She played so lovely," she said to Smitty. "It's a shame her voice was so ugly."

Jack stood up. "Anybody want pie? We have pumpkin and apple." He took orders from around the room, but Aunt Addy didn't say anything.

"Aunt Addy?" he said.

"None for me, thanks. I'm too fat as it is."

"Me too," I said. "Me neither. Do you want tea or something?" I asked her.

"Okay," she said. "I'll have that oo-thingy."

Jack brought out pie on paper plates while I started the tea. Outside it was autumn coming on winter. When it freezes outside, sometimes ice grows on the inside of the storm windows, but it wasn't freezing that day. A normal, late-autumn cold pressed against the glass. The windows fogged white, and I realized it's not the cold that does it, it's the heat from inside that clouds everything.

The room was silent except for the smacks of some of the louder eaters, Char, for instance. There should be a law. People should be taught how to eat in kindergarten: Take small bites. Keep mouth closed. Make no noises.

I pulled Dad off the piano bench, and stood him up next to me to prepare him to sing. I got out the music. "Listen, it'll be great. Since when are you shy?"

"I'm not singing," he said, and moved across the room.

There was a bit of hubbub as people jockeyed for places, argued about what to sing, or if it was better just to call it a night, but I acted like I didn't hear them. I tinkled the keys just to get warm, to see if they suggested something. I hit the first few notes of "Jingle Bells," and thought of that Joni Mitchell song that starts by singing about Christmas. It was a good trick. I started over with force so everyone would think I was really playing "Jingle Bells," then slid into the surprise.

"Smitty," Dad said over my playing. "What say we go shoot some pool?"

"Shh, Jim. Maybe later."

"C'mon. I know for sure the K of C is open tonight. I asked."

Smitty cleared his throat. I sang louder.

"We'll all go," he said to his work friends.

When I got to the part in the song about wanting a river to skate away on, I thought: Okay. Well. I realized that maybe that wasn't the best selection once I thought about the words, but I couldn't think of anything else. And I was surprised that I could play it completely from memory.

"Hey, Smitty. Think they'll let Char in?"

"Jim. C'mon."

"No, really. Char. Char! Think they'll let you in at the K of C? Sure they will."

When he started getting coats, I sang louder. No matter how loudly I played or sang, everyone talked all at once, except for Mary and Jack, who came over to sit down on either side of me. I felt the heat coming off Mary. Jack crossed a foot over his knee, tapped on his loafer with one finger. Finally, with his coat on, Dad came over too. He spread his hand down over one of mine, and pressed down until the piano clanged.

His voice was quiet, almost a whisper. "C'mon," he pleaded. When I looked up at him, he looked to Smitty and waved to signify he'd be right there. He pointed his face in the general direction of his children and still managed to avoid looking at anyone in particular. "We'll be back later," he said. He ruffled my hair as if I were a strange little neighbor kid or something.

The house emptied of people like smoke through a chimney, leaving behind only Addy, Jack, Mary, and me. Dad stood at the door zipping up his coat.

"Dad," I said. "Come back."

He looked like he was trying to swallow something, but couldn't quite move it either up and out, or safely down. "I will," he said to the wall. Then he looked at us. "I can't." He raised his hand to indicate his friends out by their cars. His face and shoulders relaxed, and I thought for a second he'd take his coat off and stay. I wanted to hug him, but as soon as I stood up, he turned.

"I'll be back later," he said as he left.

"I'm gonna go take my nap," Jack said. "I'll help with the dishes later." He dragged his skinny little self down the hall like he weighed a thousand pounds.

Mary called after him, looking at me, "I can do them when I get home." She wrapped one of Ma's best silk scarves around her neck a couple times and adjusted it without looking in a mirror.

"Where you going?" I asked.

"Out. With Jess. There's a Thanksgiving dance party downtown."

"What's his name?"

"Ben." Mary smirked. "Big Ben."

"Is he fat?" Addy asked.

Mary laughed nervously. It was rare to see her flustered. She was the cool one. "No," she said. She got into her coat quickly. "It was just a joke," she said, and left.

"*I'll* help with the dishes," Addy said, as if she *always* had to do everything.

"No. I'll do it. I haven't done anything today."

Everywhere I turned, there was food. Addy reached for the bowl of mashed potatoes, picked it up, but stopped when it was only about an inch off the table.

"Hardly any left, really," she said. "Not much even worth putting away."

I got two clean paper plates, divided the potatoes into two large portions. First, there were two plates of potatoes. And then there were none. I wasn't even hungry. Or rather, my tongue and mouth were hungry, but my stomach wasn't. I pushed past it.

I looked to see what other dishes had too little food for anyone to notice missing. Addy's back and shoulders humped forward as she ate. She sat up for a moment after the potatoes were gone, sighed. She scanned the table, did the math. I had to get her out.

"I feel sick," I said with my hands over my stomach.

"Oh, I know." She laughed, and reached for the smallest stick of stuffed celery.

"I need to move around. Please, let me clean up."

"Okay," she said, and leaned back farther into her chair.

I quickly fixed a large plate of food, wrapped it

with Saran Wrap and aluminum foil. "Here," I said. I bent down to kiss her cheek. "I'll get your coat."

She blinked a few extra beats. "Oh. Okay."

When she was finally gone, I cleared the table dish by dish. Addy was right, there wasn't that much of anything worth the trouble of putting away. I did a little at a time, washing up as I went. Corn. Peas. Char's Jell-O. None of them tasted as good as they did at dinner. I kept looking for that *one thing*. A roll? Tasted good, but no, that wasn't it. A roll with butter? That tasted better, but no, that wasn't it either. Dark meat? White meat? The other drumstick? It all went down so quickly, it was hard to tell. A roll with butter and gravy? Close. The donuts! It took two before I realized: no.

The kitchen looked ready for a new day. Then came the pain. I could hardly breathe. Why did I always do this? I lay down on the living room couch and decided I would never be unhappy like Addy. There are far too many satisfactions in life: the white of dish suds; the gleam of a clean table; the thought of where Dad would be when his buttons fell from his shirt to the floor or to the ground. That feeling between my tongue and my gut when a song came up, or the food went down.

And then I thought: If only there were chocolate. *That* might satisfy me. When I got up to look in the refrigerator to see if there was a chocolate anything, the shelves looked almost as empty as the week before. Almost no leftovers left. When I saw that, I panicked a little, but then decided that if anybody asked where all the food went, I'd tell them Addy ate it.

Interiors

Their house was small for five people, and not much to look at, but James made it a home. It was in the style of what is called a shingle house, the shingles in this case not cedar or poplar bark, but prefab, speckled blue things made of who-knows-what churned out by factories in the boom years of the 1950s and 1960s when most anyone could get a decent job and make enough money to buy one of these homes. They thought it looked very much like the drawings the children made during their first years in school: a triangular roof over a square foundation; two sets of windows in front that gave the house the appearance of having eyes; the front door like a nose between the sets of windows; and the porch under the door affording the house-face a wry smile. In reality, the porch was skewed a little to the left and had an awning overhanging it; the picture window, behind which sat the living room, was much larger in both height and width than the tripartite set of windows of the kitchen. The house may have looked like a smiling face to them, but it never looked anything like a face to me, and certainly not a smiling one.

When James married Hannah, I knew there'd be trouble. Now, twenty-five years down the line, she's dead and that house is where trouble has come to brood. The house still stands, but their home life is about as sturdy as straw. James and I have always been close, so it's only natural I should prop my younger brother up when he's weak. Being with a woman like that would weaken any man. The constant fawning and joking all the time blinds a man to the overstore of hard realities that hover over every moment of our lives. Having a wife whose lips are that busy with the bottle isn't what I would call *lucky*, but any luck James felt certain was his blew away when she died, and he buckled. He wept in public at her funeral, which I suppose is understandable, but for months afterward and sometimes even now, five months after her death, we'll be out in public somewhere—at the mall or the grocery store—and it'll happen. A song will play overhead, or he'll tweak a lemon. I don't know what goes on inside his head. He never says a word, but all of a sudden I'll look over and here comes Niagara. He doesn't just mist up; he gets all red-faced and sloppy in an effort to keep it quiet, which only makes it worse. If he weren't my brother, I'd almost be ashamed.

The kids are grown, but still live at home: Jack, 18;

Colleen, 20; Mary 21. They're headstrong and a little too tender like their father, but impetuous like their mother, which isn't the most winning combination of qualities. I know I shouldn't be fighting with a dead woman, but Lord, she's almost worse dead than she was alive. Now all I hear is *Hannah* this, *Hannah* that, *Mom, Mom, Mom*. It's enough to drive a woman batty. Lord help me, I know that's a sin. God, give me Patience. And Wisdom. And Fortitude. Even though it's my primary and most abundant gift, I find I always need more Fortitude with this bunch. "Remember," I told those kids. "We're Fallons. Buck up. Fallons are tough." Even though they're half Grace, I didn't want to mention it. They have to have a little pride.

The trouble is they all want to be *happy*, like happiness is something they can be given, or that can be taken away from them rather than what it really is: something that is made. Colleen comes home from the bank all weepy-eyed; Jack quits school, and then when I make him take that janitor job at the hospital, all he does is work, come home, and sleep. Then Mary, out at all hours with school, working part-time at that bakery, and then she says she's out "studying," but I'd bet any money she's off tathering all over town with those strange friends of hers with the weird getups and hairdos—even the boys.

But with a mother like that, what can you expect?

She was weak as water, not a good example. I suppose she was smart enough, but in all the wrong ways. No sense. You can't drink like that and think it won't catch up with you. "A big snow and black ice," James says when he tells people how she died, but it could have been sunshine and apple blossoms for all that. Drunk driving is drunk driving no matter the weather.

What this family really needs to pull it together is *events*, and the Miniature Makers Confabulation at Cobo Hall is the perfect thing. Even though none of them came last year when I won Honorable Mention, this year will be different. A good home needs a strong woman at the center of it. If I have to be the glue that holds this family together, then so be it, I'll be the glue. My house is made of brick.

On the farm, when we were young, things were different. Mother died when James was only fifteen. I fought with Pa tooth and nail to let me finish high school, but he wanted me to take over Ma's chores on the farm. It was rough, but I held my ground. After Ma died, Pa's drinking got bad. He got mean, and I knew that, much as I hated the idea of James there alone, if I didn't leave, I'd never get out. So, when I heard that Eunice O'Shaughnessy's dentist brother needed help in his office in Detroit, I jumped at the chance. I wrote Ma Phelan to secure a room in her boardinghouse, and I was off. I switched jobs after a year, moving over to Dr. Harrington's office because I wanted to work with a real doctor, not just a dentist. I sent money back to Pa for the farm to justify my leaving, but wrote separately to James, stuffing a few dollars in for him, and told him to save it and be sure Pa didn't make him quit school. Pa was a mean drunk, but he never hit us, although sometimes a word is harder to take than the back of a hand.

Then, when Pa died and James came to live with me in Detroit, things weren't just okay, they were grand. It was the best time of our lives. Detroit was really alive in the fifties. We went out almost every night. We ate, we danced, we sang.

And then he met Hannah.

She used that tinge of Irish accent to charm people, but it didn't work on me. Sure, her parents came over on the boat, but she was born here in Detroit, so whenever you heard the hard *t*, the burr on an *r*, or an extra lilt for emphasis, you could be sure it was a put-on. Our family and the whole third of Huron County where James and I grew up were Irish immigrants, so she wasn't putting anything over on me.

"I love him, Addy," she said to me when I asked just what she thought she was doing. "And he loves me." Then she put that look on her face like she was *sorry* for me. "I know you don't understand, but we're in love. It's the best thing."

"Oh, I understand. I understand plenty." I looked her up and down to let her know I had her full measure, and then I walked away. She seemed to have gotten the notion that because I'd put on a few pounds and made no secret about the fact that I brooked no nonsense from men, I somehow didn't know this about that.

At the harvest dances on the farm, there was plenty of that going around. I was just a girl then and James was too young to go, so I'd go with a whole troupe of people from the neighboring farms. Oh, the boys. They'd dance with you for a few dances, invite you for a drive afterward, get you all moonshined up, and the next thing you know, you're in somebody's field flat on a horse blanket over dewy grass, cows lowing not so far off and him huffing and sighing above you. Then all you're left with is wet, ruined shoes, a memory of rank manure and hay, a good measure of discomfort for days after, and worry for weeks after that. But of course, that's how half the county got born. Most girls just weren't that smart.

I only ever did it with Seamus Doyle because he said he loved me and I was fool enough to think I loved him too, with all his palaver. "Look at the stars," he used to say to distract me. But who cares about starlight? They're just white spots that litter the sky and have nothing to do with me. Next thing I know, Seamus takes up with that Schultz girl from the German part of the county, although if it happened now, I'd have never wasted a tear over her. She got round and tight as a pumpkin, and when I told her older brothers it was Seamus, they gave him a proper thrashing. It serves him right for not staying with his own kind. *Look at the stars*, to be sure. It was enough to put me off the sky completely.

I was just a thin little slip of a thing myself back then, but I never used it as a trap for men. I can take care of myself, and I was sure to let men know it. Men will tell you a bunch of malarkey to get what they want, then suddenly you're no use to them at all, or they think you're their slave. I was always too smart for that. Even Paul Hess, with his *marry me, marry me* during the first few years after James married Hannah. Paul tried to win me over with his *sensitivity*. I felt it was either a trick or he was too soft. He never gave me a challenge, never had the ambition a man should have. Still, I never thought he'd leave. Anyway, it doesn't matter. He wasn't Irish. He wasn't even Catholic.

I had Hannah's number from the first. When James brought her home to meet me, she sat there all stringy neck and jutting collarbones the way skinny women do, and I just knew she'd be the type who had to have a man on her arm to show the world. Hanging all over James right in front of me all *Oh, look at me with my heart on my sleeve.* Well, I thought, *That's why God gave us skin, so we wouldn't have to look at the bloody mess that's inside us, and that's how we should keep it.* Overemotional people like that just don't cut it with me. She wasn't the type to be alone. She wasn't strong enough for it.

"She's very talented, Addy," James said. When I purposely didn't ask, *At what?* he went on about her playing guitar, piano, accordion, what have you. But sit next to her during a church hymn or a round of "Happy Birthday," and it'd just about cripple your ear to hear her. She couldn't sing worth a lick. How can it be that someone who can play so well has a voice like a kicked cat?

James has a soft spot in him fathoms deep and a mile wide, and I knew if anyone uncovered it, he'd be lost. We've all got it, don't we, but I learned to patch mine over before I left the farm. No one should have to feel that way, and I wasn't going to be fool enough to let it happen again. I saw it happening to him and I did my best to stop it. "Find someone sensible," I told him. "It's a contract. You need someone to trust, someone who will do for you as well as you do for her. If you pollute your head with that mushy stuff, then you're lost. Lovey-dovey isn't real. When it clears away like smoke, all you're left with is a sting in the eye and a bad taste in your mouth. Listen to that awful stirring inside and you'll regret it all your life."

But he wouldn't listen. Now all those kids have the same look, that same yearning for nothing definite that can only lead to a world of trouble and unhappiness all your life. Well, everyone wants something beautiful to come into their lives, don't they? The difference with me is I take control and *make* beauty. I don't depend on anyone else and never have. I don't understand how anyone can be happy otherwise.

I built a small Irish village last year complete with thatched roofs, sheep grazing in mossy green pastures, even a peat bog. This year I'm moving to interiors.

Honorable Mention is an accomplishment, so I have nothing to be disappointed about. That was only my second year at the Miniature Makers Confabulation, and who'd've dreamed I'd even make the finals? I think the reason I didn't place higher was that they made the mistake of valuing perfection over realism, but I'm not about to compromise my artistic integrity just for a prize. Although I admit I could have planned better—the clay in my bog didn't travel well in the July heat, and it got a bit soupy by the time I'd set it all up in the poorly air-conditioned corner of Cobo Hall where they stashed us. Honorable Mention in all of Southeast Michigan is nothing to sneeze at. We Fallons were made for big things. Next year I might even try for the Nationals. I'm sure I'm good enough.

Interiors are a whole different world. The problem is finding something interesting to show. Anyone can do a quaint kitchen tableau, but quaint isn't really my style. I thought instead I would do a doctor's office the way I'd want it to look if it were completely up to me. You'd be amazed what you can do with a good batch of balsa wood, paper, glue, toothpicks, and Popsicle sticks. And, of course, paint. But you can't just slap together some toothpicks and Popsicle sticks and call it a chair. I do research, and then replicate Chippendale, Shaker, French Colonial, or what have you. I build them with the raw materials, then re-create the style by hand using ultra-fine cutting tools. It requires intense precision and patience.

And then it's not just the furniture and the story content, but the décor. I'm doing it all in variations on plaid. I wanted something to reflect the complicated fabric of our lives that is revealed in a very personal way in a doctor's office, and I thought, what's more complicated than plaid? I tried describing it to Dr. Harrington as a possibility for our own office, but he laughed as if it were a joke. What he didn't seem to get was that I didn't mean the usual kind of plaid. It would be all new color combinations, muted, and very subtle.

The whole thing is set on sturdy eleven-by-seventeen pasteboard. Of course, I built the doctor's back office, and my office right next to it with a tiny desk and chair just like mine, except I've made my chair Louis Quatorze and the desk French Colonial. I've devoted each exam room to a different disease. The world is full of misery and suffering, so the problem was how to narrow it down to only three interesting maladies. If people knew all the disgusting, embarrassing predicaments of the human condition I've been witness to as Dr. Harrington's assistant . . . Anyway, that was in the early days, before he felt he needed a nurse with a degree to help him with the patients and changed my job to office manager.

I call my tableau "Internal Medicine." I have a room in dark brown and orange plaid with stirrups, a speculum on the exam table, and an IV pole. I filled the deep red/lemon yellow plaid room with crutches, splints, casts, bandages. In the last room, which I made lime green and purple plaid, I put tiny cotton swabs, a freeze gun, scalpels, Petri dishes, specimen jars, a tiny to-scale chart of the internal workings of the male and female reproductive systems. I may have to break down and put people in the exam rooms, but

I'm afraid that would be putting too fine a point on it. Wouldn't it? A pregnant woman in the stirrups, a child with a broken arm, a small man with a very worried expression? And in the pale-blue-and-white waiting room, a husband, parents, and a friend among the empty chairs. But I'm not too good with people.

I would never claim it for myself, but by all accounts, I'm considered extremely organized and efficient, so I try to put my considerable gifts to good use. I helped James arrange everything when she died, calling the funeral home, writing the obituary and calling it into the paper, arranging the Mass and every last detail of the funeral. I even ordered the headstone. James and the kids would have settled for one of those piddly little flat things, but when I got wind of that, I took over. I may not have seen eye to eye with her on everything, but she was my sister-in-law, and I thought she should for once have something with a little bit of class. "Just leave it to me," I told them and I ushered them all out of the room. It took a while to get everything organized, and to be honest, I forgot about it a little bit until James reminded me after the second or third month, but the stone mason people called me last week to confirm the inscription and said that it should be done in less than a month and placed on the grave shortly thereafter.

In the middle of all that, I had the move from the apartment to my new house. The kids hold it against me that James gave me a little of the insurance money to help me buy this house. It's not like it's a mansion or anything, but here in Livonia I'm much closer to them than I was in that dingy apartment all the way over on the east side. Plus, I need the extra room to make my miniatures—another thing they don't understand. That's okay. I don't expect them to understand art, but it pains me sometimes to see them squander their lives.

I made Jack go back to Schoolcraft College to get his GED, not that he necessarily needs it to clean toilets in a hospital. And him, smart as a whip. The smartest of the bunch, I'd say. If only he'd apply himself, he could really be something. Since Hannah died, he walks around like a ghost, but sometimes Mary will put her clanging music on and he'll up and dance his heart out like in the old days. He moves like the best I've seen even on *Dance Fever*, although it's a little embarrassing the way he wiggles and jiggles all over the place, but as long as it's just in their living room, what does it hurt? James was a lovely dancer when we were younger, but in those days, men moved more solid and strong. I guess all that changed with Elvis, and nowadays who knows what the kids are into? Dancing is one thing, but you can't make a career out of that. He's my favorite, but he worries me.

Colleen's another story altogether. Mean as a bear sometimes, but at least she was smart enough to take the bank job I arranged for her with my friend Virginia.

And you can't tell anything to that Mary; she'll just smile you right down like a cat.

"Mary," I said to her, thinking there's no way she'd get out of it if I cornered her. "I got you a job at Dr. O'Shaughnessy's son's office. I worked for his father when I first came to Detroit, so they know me well. They know I wouldn't recommend any flakes. He's a dentist, not a real doctor like where I work, but it's a good place for a young woman to start. I've set everything up. Call this number and you can probably start next week. But you can figure that out between yourselves when you call."

"Oh, Aunt Addy," she says in that polite way she has. "That's very nice of you, but I have a job."

"Yes, but this a *good* job."

"I'm okay."

"I don't think you understand," I said. "I got you this job on the strength of my good name."

"That's so sweet. Thank you. But I'm the weekend manager at the bakery. Mrs. Hennessey depends on me."

"De*pends* on you. She'll get along just dandy without you, believe you me."

"And I like it. But tell them thank you, and that I'm sorry it didn't work out." Then she pulls on that odd little red bolero jacket in her smooth, swift way, kisses my cheek, and out she walks. "Gotta go. Bye." Just like that.

"That's my good name," I called after her, but she ignored me. You can't go around working at jobs just because you "like" them. You have to think of your future sometime. She put me in a very uncomfortable position. What was I supposed to say, "I went to all this trouble to arrange everything, but my niece is a flake and would rather work in a bakery"? Well, if she's a flake, then she is. It doesn't come from my side of the family.

I'm incredibly self-sufficient, but if I don't specifically ask James for a favor, sometimes a whole week can go by without my seeing him.

"How's my James?" I ask him on one of the Saturdays when he comes over to fooster with the windows to get the air conditioner to fit. It's late August and hot as all get-out, and even though there's only a month or so left of the heat, I can't stand it with just a fan.

He said now that Hannah's gone, he doesn't need

the air conditioner in their bedroom, that I can have it. Of course, I refused, but he said, "You don't realize how much heat another body next to you generates, until it's gone."

"Well, if you insist," I said. It's the least I could do for him.

After he hauled the air conditioner in the house and set it under the window, I handed him the card.

MINIATURE MAKERS
CONFABULATION
COBO HALL
DETROIT, MICHIGAN
SATURDAY, SEPTEMBER 20, 1980

"I think it'd be a good thing for everybody to come. A nice family outing. It's time we started acting like a real family. Nobody does anything together anymore. It's not right, James. It's not natural."

He put the card in his back pocket without saying anything, as is his way. I knew I'd have to prod him if I wanted to get anything out of him.

"Oh, I almost forgot!" I said. "They called and said the headstone will be ready to place that very week of the Confab. But isn't that perfect! We can make a day of it. We'll go to the cemetery in the morning, then I'll go set up at the Confab, and you all can come later, in time for the prizes. Afterward, we can all go to five o'clock Mass. I'll call Father Walsh to make sure that night's Mass is said for Hannah. So, it's all set."

He hoisted the air conditioner into the window and, after a lot of grunting, secured it. By the time he'd finished, he was just dripping. He's always been sinewy and lean, but I thought he was looking more gaunt lately. Sometimes it just kills me to look at him, I love him so much.

I couldn't help myself and I said, "I'm lucky to have you, James." I kissed his forehead, but it was salty and damp with sweat. Yes, it was disgusting, but he is my brother, so I just politely excused myself before going to the bathroom to spit and wash my face.

After work one night, I dropped by to tell them the dates of the Mini Confab so they could clear their calendars. James was gone as usual; Jack and Mary had gone shopping. James is so busy and sometimes forgets, so I brought a little flyer I had printed up to pin to their corkboard in the kitchen. I wanted it to be there as a gentle reminder. I didn't want to harp at them too much about it, and I refuse to beg.

"Why didn't you go shopping with Mary and Jack?" I asked Colleen.

"We don't have the same taste. Plus, I don't like

the music they play in the car. It should be called 'junk rock' instead of punk rock."

"No," I said. "Music isn't what it used to be."

"I'm making pasta with red sauce. Hungry?"

"Well, sure," I said, just to humor her. She fancies herself a gourmet like her mother did. "But not too much garlic. My sensitive stomach."

"We have leftover chicken. Do you want me to add some of that to the sauce? Or maybe clams?"

"You don't have any ground beef? Well, chicken sounds fine, I guess."

She plopped a glass bowl on the kitchen table with a big lump of something that looked like yellow clay inside. I almost didn't want to know, but I asked what it was anyway.

"The pasta," she says. "I made it fresh. It's easy. Flour, eggs, a little olive oil."

"Well. How about that. It's very . . . yellow, isn't it. You certainly are creative." I let my compliment sit for a minute before I added, "You know, we're a very creative family. We surely are. You with your singing and cooking. James sings so lovely too. And your mother played so many instruments, just like you."

"She taught us."

"Your father sings so well, and your mother played so well, and you do both."

"I guess I'm a weird combination of Mom and Dad."

"Well, I *always* thought it was a weird combination."

She got that wounded, mean look she gets, just like her mother, and I thought maybe I shouldn't have said that out loud, but it was done, and there's no use lying.

"You know, Ma was always nice to you as far as I could see. What's your problem with her?"

She's a sharp-tongued little snipe, but this night I was hoping she'd have left the fight somewhere else. It's my duty as her aunt to put her in her place.

"We were always raised to respect our elders, Colleen. I would never say something so forward to my father's sister. I was just now praising Hannah's talent, so you should let it rest there."

That shut her up, so I went on. "I was praising the whole family's talents. Jack too. He sings and plays too. He's loaded with talent. And his dancing! He's a regular Deney Terrio, although sometimes it looks a little too swishy for my taste. I'll talk to him about that."

"Welp," she says. "I wouldn't do that."

Now, she knew very well I wasn't asking what *she* would do about anything, but I drew on my Fortitude and let it slide. Although I did know what she meant. As flinty as James can be, Jack is more like a diamond: Finely honed. Beautiful, but hard. He's my favorite for a reason: a true Fallon. He makes you almost afraid to criticize. Say something he doesn't like and he'll get quiet, lift his patient, handsome face to you until whatever you just said comes bouncing right back at you as if you were the one in the wrong. There's a danger in his silences. He'll make a girl a fine husband someday, just like his father. I hope he chooses someone more on his level than what James got. If James and Jack are flint and diamond, this girl is pudding, all soft and squishy with her emotions. Hannah, of course, was cheap red wine spilled on a white carpet, just a mess.

And Mary. I don't know about that girl. I just don't get her at all.

"And Mary," I said. "Well, Mary. She's . . . she *is* very creative. With her clothes. She wears such . . . *unusual* things. Well, she's so pretty, she could throw on a potato sack and make it look good, couldn't she?"

Colleen laughed, which was a relief.

"And you know, not to brag, but I have a few talents myself."

Colleen looked at me and waited. I could see she wasn't going to offer, so I continued.

"My miniatures," I said. "For which I got an Honorable Mention at last year's Mini Confab."

"Oh, right."

"I know none of you could come last year. It was a bit last minute, wasn't it? I just found out the date for this year's. It's been pushed off to September, which is good. Last year's in July, it was just so hot."

"That's good."

"Yes," I said. "September twentieth. It's a Saturday. I wanted to let you all know so you could plan this year. I think your mother had some other thing you all had to do last year, or something."

"Oh. Okay, well," she said. She slapped the yellow lump on the table, rolled it out, and folded it over again and again. "I'll let everyone know. But you know, I don't know. Mary starts school again in September, and Jack just started his job at Sinai, so he may not be able to get off so soon, being new and all."

"But it's on a weekend."

"He asked to work every weekend because there are fewer people around."

"That's very odd. My, these cookies are wonderful. Are they store bought or did you make them?"

"I made them."

"They're *very* good. I'm surprised. You'd think someone like Jack would want to be around people more, not less. I think that's very odd."

She shrugged.

"Well, I'm glad I came over, then. I'm glad it's still a month away; that way you can all plan for it."

"And Dad. I don't know what he'll be up to." She was sweating now with all the folding and rolling the lump flat. Not very attractive at all. She got out a long knife and cut the dough into long, thin strips. She lifted the strips and let them drop in a tangle onto floury wax paper, then went to deal with the bubbling red sauce on the stove. She stirred it absently and said, "Aunt Addy, do you know what the deal is with Dad?"

"The deal?" The way these kids talk.

"What does he do? Where does he go? Why isn't he ever home?" She said all this with her back turned to me, as if the sauce would answer her. Then she comes out with, "Do you think there's a *woman*?"

"Good God! What makes you think that?"

"He's gone all the time."

"Oh God. He *is* a pretty soft touch. He falls into that lovey-dovey stuff and there's no saving him from himself." This would be terrible if it's true. After a few nibbles on another cookie, I said, "No. It simply can't be. If it's true, we can't allow it. But he *can't* be that foolish." I finished the cookie and then realized, "But this is exactly what I'm talking about. We all need to start doing things together. If I know James—and nobody knows him better than I do—he's off sulking somewhere by himself. That was always his way as a boy, until I would corral him and bring him back into the fold. And that's what we have to do now. Ha. It's funny how people basically never change. We'll spend the whole day together at the Mini Confab, and it can be a whole new start. We'll make it a Family Day. The first of many. You'll see. Really."

"What makes you think he'll come?"

"I'll take care of everything. Like I always do."

"In a way it's like he died, too." She turned the red sauce down to simmer, and when the pot of water next to it began to boil, she gathered the strips of pasta and dropped them all into the water. "It's been five months since Ma died. I just . . . I keep waiting for things to get back to normal. Well. I guess there *is* no normal without Ma. And then, without Dad too. It's just . . . It's lonely."

And then she starts with the waterworks again, feeling sorry for herself like she's the only one who's ever lost a mother. I could just slap her. She minds the pasta, tossing it occasionally with salad tongs, dripping tears all down her face. That's going to be some salty pasta, I think, but of course I don't say anything. *What do you know about lonely*, I want to ask. I know all about lonely. Coming to Detroit all by myself, not a soul to help me. Those few sweet years with me and James living the life, then all that ended when Hannah pranced onto the scene, and I've been lonely ever since. I want to explain how two people—a brother and a sister—can live happy as larks and not be lonely. Add a third person and it makes you lonelier than you ever thought possible. Add to that all the empty fakery of men, and what are you left with but a table full of dirty dishes and a gnawing emptiness that nothing can fill. But I don't say anything. I let her have her maudlin little scene to herself. I'm dog tired from working all day, but I get up anyway and get the plates and forks and napkins to set the table. I scout the fridge for something to drink, pour us both a glass, and tell her they're almost out of milk.

The Saturday before the Confab, I called James over to help me move some furniture around. When the kids helped during the move, they plopped the furniture any which way they thought looked good enough, and I just don't live like that. They fashioned the couch and two chairs into a circle around the glass coffee table, but I think it works better if all the seats are side by side so I can see out the picture window. If someone decides to peep into my windows at night, I want to be sure to see him before he sees me. James, of course, won't let me help with the heavy stuff because he knows how frail I am. The doctor says I need to get up and move around more, but he doesn't understand. I move around plenty at work trying to keep everything under control in his office. Plus, sometimes it takes more energy to sit for hours on end working on my miniatures than to jump rope or whatever silly thing he thinks I should do to take off the weight. My minis require extreme concentration. It's exhausting. I make whole perfect little worlds. You'd think an educated man like the doctor would understand art, but apparently not.

James is wiry, but strong, and he did what I told him with the furniture in no time.

The thread at the bottom edge of his T-shirt had unstrung, and the extra material unraveled, leaving a frayed, tattered droop about two inches along the seam. When everything was finally in its rightful place, I pinched his shirt and pulled it away from his body to show him. "James, we really do need to go shopping to get some new clothes for you. You used to be so persnickety about your appearance."

"Cheap things," he said. "I just bought this. That's okay, Coll will fix it. She's very handy with the needle and thread."

"The kids tell me you're gone a lot lately," I venture.

"It helps to keep busy."

"Busy is fine, James, but . . . James, you know me. You know I can't dilly dally. Is there something else going on? Somewhere else you're going?"

He worked his hands over his face as if he'd rub it off.

"Look. I'm working a lot, okay? It helps."

"James, there's no need to spend every free moment with your kids if you don't want to. In fact, I think it's good for you to have more time to yourself. Just check in every once in a while. And I'm always here to go over and check on them. I can see how being around them might remind you too much of Hannah. The kids are older now. We were taking care of ourselves at their age, remember? They'd probably resent it if you were hovering around them all the time anyway. But I'm different. Don't be a stranger to *me*, of all people. You can come over here whenever you need to get away from all the reminders of home. It's completely understandable. It might help if you got rid of some of Hannah's stuff. It's been almost six months now, after all. Why torture yourself with memories? Just don't . . . confuse yourself by getting mixed up in . . . other things."

He'd been screwing magnets into the cupboards to make sure they close as tightly as I like. I hate the thought of ants getting into my honey and such. He tested them over and over needlessly while I talked, but he stopped when I stopped and he looked at me, his hand leaning against the cupboard.

"So that's the truth, then, James? You're working a lot?"

He looked irritated with me, turned his palms up,

and cocked his head a little as if to say, *What do you want from me?* I wanted to ask if there was a woman, but here is where my Fortitude failed me. It made me uncomfortable just to say the word, and if it wasn't true, then I didn't want to put ideas into his head.

"Well, of course, I don't mind, but the kids wanted me to ask." He shook his head a little, and then I had an idea. "Do you know what? I'm going to call that boss of yours to talk to him. It's not good for you to work so much."

He started to laugh and wouldn't stop. He got himself practically into a fit.

"I don't see what's so funny," I said, but he wouldn't stop laughing and shaking his head.

"Addy," he said when he finally gathered a little breath. "No forty-seven-year-old man needs his sister to call his boss for him. Don't be ridiculous."

"You'll be my little brother until the day I die. Nothing will change that, James. Like it or not."

Then all of a sudden, without any warning, he starts talking, but almost in a whisper, like he's afraid of something.

"You know, Hannah was a big reader."

I didn't get the connection, so I sat down and waited for him to continue, and he sat too.

"None of us ever went to college . . ."

"You don't have to go to college to be smart, James. Everybody knows that . . ."

He cut his hand up into the air between us with his palm facing me, which he's never done before.

"I don't want you interrupting me," he said, still in a deadly whisper.

Hmpph.

"We've got walls and walls of books in our bedroom. She had some of the teachers at work give her lists of books to read. It was like an addiction."

Among others.

"A few months ago, I was moving stuff around and one of the books fell. I opened it up, and there was Hannah's handwriting. She wrote all over these books. Sometimes it's just underlines, but occasionally she wrote whole thoughts all up and down the edges of the page. I started reading her books, just to know what she was thinking about. It was almost like talking to her again."

"That's a little morbid." He didn't stop me, so I pushed ahead, because someone had to say it. "She's dead, James. I know it sounds hard, but it's time to move on."

"You think it's ridiculous, don't you? Reading her books."

"Yes," I had to admit. "Seems sort of a waste of time too."

"Hannah always said there were different kinds of strength. She said you confused being strong with being hard. I think she was right."

He stood, looked over the chairs, and repositioned them at a little angle to the couch.

"No," I said. "They should be straight. Everything should be in a straight line."

He straightened the line of chairs and said, "Hannah always said *you* should run for president." He laughed again, but I never got Hannah's sense of humor, and I guess not all that much has changed.

I had James load my "Internal Medicine" tableau into my car last night so I wouldn't have to rush this morning. I was a little nervous. I had a hard time sleeping last night. I knew I shouldn't have ordered that pizza for dinner. I was just going to have two pieces and then save the rest for lunch during the week, but it was so good, and I was so nervous, and then next thing I knew, it was gone. It sat like a rock in my stomach all night and gave me terrible pizza dreams.

I told them I thought it was important we all go together as a family to see Hannah's stone, but since I needed to get down to Cobo Hall by eight o'clock to set up, we had to get up at sparrow fart this morning to fit in the visit to the cemetery. The light was just breaking as we pulled in. I was in the lead, and it took a little while because all I had was the plot number. I didn't hear James beeping when I passed it, but eventually we got there. The ground was very squishy, and I wished I had brought another pair of shoes to wear downtown.

Finally, we found the plot, and there it was,
upright like a proper head stone, beautifully arched
at the top with an understated finial on each corner.

Hannah Fallon (née Grace)
June 16, 1934 – March 24, 1980
Wife, Mother, Sister-in-Law

I'd opted out of the word "Devoted" in the last line. It seemed too much, and I thought more fleur-de-lis around the border would be better. I held my breath waiting for the waterworks to start, but nothing happened for a long time. I didn't want to gawk, so I purposely had my shoulder turned so they could cry or hold each other or whatever. I stared off at the pond beyond the hill thinking about my office tableau sitting in the back of my car, hoping the glue would hold and I could get it safely to Cobo Hall without jostling it around too much in the car. First Place. Wouldn't that be lovely.

The cemetery is a strange wilderness surrounded

by suburbs and the city. A line of ducks gathered at the edge of a mossy pond. Then, of all things, a long, thin stick of a bird with a huge wingspan that looked like something prehistoric lifted out of the weeds on the other side of the pond. A blue heron, maybe. Suddenly, Colleen says, "I can't believe it." I turned then, and instead of them looking at the beautiful new headstone, or the blue heron, they were all looking at me like I don't know what.

"It's very pretty, isn't it," I said.

James said, "Addy."

Jack wouldn't look at me, and stood shaking his head at his loafers. Mary had no politeness left in her face, and Colleen stomped off to the car and slammed the door. Their emotions had obviously gotten the best of them, but even if they weren't particularly fond of the style I'd chosen, I thought I at least deserved a thank-you for all my effort. Since it was clear I wouldn't get one, I thought it would be best to just wrap it up quickly there and move along before my office tableau melted. I tried to think of a diplomatic way to get the show on the road, but then James said, "Hannah's birthday was June tenth. Not June sixteenth."

"Well."

What he said sounded right.

"James, I asked you for all the information before

I ordered the stone. I wrote it all down." To prove it, I rooted through my purse to find it, and there it was plain as day, in my own handwriting. I showed it to James. Granted, when looked at a certain way, that 6 *could* have looked like a 0 with a cowlick at the top, but that's a mistake anyone could have made.

"You celebrated her birthday every year with us for the past twenty-five years, Addy."

And, of course, despite the evidence of my note card, I realized a terrible mistake had been made.

"Well," I said. "I mean . . ."

I'd written it down, and it was an indisputable fact that I could see. It was a number. The date I carried around in my head for her birthday was also an indisputable fact. But somehow the two indisputable facts never met in my head. The number on the page was a number, and the date in my head was an idea, and I never thought to compare them to see if one was wrong. I mean, who would? I never make mistakes. But you'd think they'd be able to understand that I am only human.

"It's just a date, James."

We really needed to get going. It was seven o'clock, and I needed to get downtown by eight at the latest to set up. The cool of dawn was already giving way to the heat of the last summer day. Colleen was the only one who hadn't driven her own car, and now she laid on the horn to get Jack to come. Jack and Mary turned to go, then so did James.

"I don't know how this happened," I said. He looked at me as if I'd done it on purpose or something. "But don't worry, I'll fix it. You can be sure I'll make it right."

They all kept walking.

"I'll see you all there at ten o'clock or so, okay? My table is G4. If you wanted to come early, that'd be fine too," I said. "And I'll take care of everything with this thing here. First thing Monday, I'll call." They were getting so far away. I had a hard time walking on that soft ground, and I get out of breath much more easily than when I was younger. My shoes seemed to sink so much farther down into the dirt than theirs did. I wasn't sure they could still hear me, so I had to raise my voice. "It's a mistake," I said again as they got into their cars, but I was out of breath and I'm sure they didn't hear. I almost said, "It's not like it's a matter of life and death or anything," but I caught myself.

The traffic downtown was horrendous. I had the air-conditioning on full blast, but I was sweating like a Roman soldier and I was afraid I'd get the seat damp again. I had the towel I keep on the seat there, but I had to fooster around to get my skirt up so there'd be no sweat spot on my behind, as has happened before.

Lord, why all these burdens? I mean, I know everyone has burdens, but why have you given me these particular burdens: The extra weight, the overactive glands, the ill health, my extreme organizational skills that everyone seems to resent? And then this family. You blessed me many times over with James, but then gave him away to this family who seem like strangers to me. I feel homesick all the time. And now I've hurt James, as a result of your Great Plan, whatever that might be. He has suffered so much already, but why make him suffer at *my* hand? How could I be so stupid? Best not to think about it.

I got to Cobo Hall much later than I'd hoped. I had a hard time finding a cart to transport my tableau from the car to my booth, but eventually I had everything in place by nine o'clock. The judging wouldn't begin until eleven, but I wanted a good chance to walk around with the family to look at the competition. I was between two women I'd never met before. On my right was a young woman with a husband and baby. The husband seemed to do everything for her, from the setup to feeding the baby. Before long, four or five of his brothers and sisters or cousins or whatever showed up to crowd around her display. They got to be so many, I had to ask them to move away so they wouldn't block my tableau. The lady to my left was my age. I don't know who the young fellow was who helped her set up, but as soon as he'd gone off to wander around, she started in with the questions.

"Yes," I said. "My family should be here shortly. James and his kids."

"Is that your son and grandkids?"

"No. I've never married."

"Oh," she said, and then she stopped like so many people do, as if I were a freak of some sort, or a danger.

"Good luck," she said, and that was the last word from her. I told her good luck too, and by the look of her display, she'd need it. Another quaint kitchen and living room scene painted pretty colors.

I didn't want to walk around to look at the other tableaux in case I missed James and the kids, but by ten thirty I thought maybe I'd better or I wouldn't get another chance. I knew they'd find me. Perhaps one of the kids' cars broke down or something, or maybe James was called into work unexpectedly. I'm sure there's a good reason.

The competition is even tougher this year than I expected, but it cheers me to see how some people have grown in their artistic development. Of course, there's the predictable battlefield crowd, which take up most of the show room. I wouldn't have recognized any of them if they weren't labeled—the Antietams, a couple of Gettysburgs, three different Bunker Hills, mostly blood and mud, not very interesting at all.

In interiors, this seems to be the year of the café. There's a very well-done Parisian café, which doesn't really seem fair, since half of it is technically not an interior. There's another one called "Night Café," with a Vincent van Gogh poster next to it: very clever, and the colors are strange and perfect. This might be one to worry about, but because it's a copy from a painting and not an original idea it should have points deducted.

At eleven, I take my place behind my table and watch the other families arrive. Cobo Hall is quite large. Perhaps James and the kids got lost in here. They could be wandering around looking for me right now. Or maybe something else came up. Well, that's all right. I understand. Really, I'm just happy to sit here and watch the crowd. It's mostly families, husbands, wives, kids. I suppose it's just my imagination, but it feels like they've given me one of the worst spots. The lights overhead are so bright and hot, I can't imagine they would show anything off to good advantage. It's good lighting for showing off the miniatures, but not so good for live people. It washes out the faces, shows off all the lines and dry skin, which makes me thankful I've at least always had a good complexion.

If there were more time, I'd complain, but I wouldn't like to call attention to myself this late in the game.

It's good to be out in the world, seeing all the different types of people. Everyone here has someone to talk to. I listen in, and mostly they're not talking about anything; a bad day, a good meal, some story about a wrong turn, nothing at all. They can talk about nothing at all, and it's nice. Sometimes that's all anybody really needs.

The judges have started. They march out in a line and parade around to each table, stop, jot down notes, and move along. I've set out my placard on the tabletop and taped another so that it hangs off the edge:

Adelaide Fallon
G4
"Internal Medicine"

The buzz of the other families grows louder. I should have brought a book. Well, at least everyone seems happy; that's what a family should be, and it strikes me that that's the problem right there: James married an unhappy woman. One must at least try to be happy. The secret to my happiness is that I'm always doing for others. I never give a thought to myself.

There should be a rule that only the creator can be at the table when the judges come around. When people have their whole posse there, it gets crowded and distracting. I'm getting a little nervous. I'd love to take home a First Prize trophy to James and the kids to show them. Maybe this will be my year.

When the judges get to the third table down from me, I look up and all the way across the room near the battlefields I spot that silly daisy bag Colleen drags around with her everywhere. It is. It's James and all three kids, but they don't see me. "My family," I say to the lady on my left, and then I say it again to the family on the right.

They still haven't seen me. The kids' faces are hard and sour, but I think they'll enjoy themselves once they get a chance to look around. They'll find we have much more in common than they suspected. This could awaken in them a sense of the true Fallon Spirit. A sense of possibility. I can imagine reading about it in a fan magazine years from now, when Colleen, with that fantastic voice of hers, becomes a svelte chanteuse, and thanks her Aunt Addy for being a shining example. Or Jack arrives at a premier as the leading actor in a movie. His new wife is a pretty young starlet next to him on the red carpet, and someone with a microphone asks him when it all started for him, and he tells all about me, about today, and how he hadn't realized what he had inside him until my example unleashed it for him. I could see Mary with a fine husband and family. They'll thank me later. So much that turns wonderful begins as a hard kernel of pain. Silly nothings like water and air can kick it into bloom, like that mustard seed in the Bible. Perhaps my example today will do the trick. Oh Lord, please. It does my heart good.

"My family is here." I can't go greet them because the judges are drawing closer, but I stand up to get a better vantage. James still hasn't seen me, so I start to wave. "My family," I say again, but nobody is listening. We're all together.

Poor James looks more gaunt than ever. Jack looks tired, and Mary looks distracted. Colleen sees me first. She doesn't say anything to James. She stares daggers at me, but I have faith this will be the day everything will change. I will be their mustard seed that makes it all better. Let it be me. Thank you, Lord.

A man touches James on the arm and points to the "Interiors" sign. James follows the man's finger, turns to thank him. I wave again as the judges arrive at my table.

Love is a little bit of magic, isn't it. As if we were connected by an invisible force, my heart lifts when James's hand lifts, and he waves.

Harmony

Our Jack answered the door when the police came that raw, late March evening so many years ago. The temperature dropped all through the day and the rain turned to snow. Still a senior in high school, Jack was the youngest of us three. "Is this the home of Hannah Fallon?" the police asked him.

"Yes," Jack said. Nobody else was home. Dad was working overtime; I was still at the bakery. Colleen had already closed out her teller's window at the bank and left for home; she'd find out soon enough. The snow dropped thick and fast.

"This is Officer Nichols. I'm Officer Clemons. Could we come in?"

"No," Jack said.

He made them stand on the porch rubbing their hands together as the fat flakes dusted their shoulders, even though it was almost spring. They slipped a card with the Sixteenth Precinct's number written on it under the aluminum storm door, which Jack had locked. He wouldn't give them Dad's work number either, so they told him to have Dad call them when he got home. They'd meet him at Mount Carmel Hospital.

"Mary, it's Jack," he told me over the phone. "Mom had an accident. Come home now." I found out later he said the same thing to Dad. When she walked through the front door, before she even had a chance to kick off her shoes, he told Colleen what the police said: That our ma was driving, and they thought she'd been drinking. That she'd lost control of the car on Outer Drive and crashed. He was the first of us to say it. "Colleen," he said, "I think she's dead."

That was so long ago, a world away, Detroit, 1980. I had taken to wearing brightly colored clothing—lime green, purple, orange—to offset the ubiquitous gray and brown of Detroit. When Ma and Dad thought I was at the movies or studying late at the library, I went instead to dance at Bookies on West McNichols, a gay bar that played punk and new wave music, and all I really cared about then was what I was wearing, what new punk or new wave band out of London I'd hear, what guy I might meet next.

Aunt Addy came back to the house from the hospital with Dad. Ever-present with her nose into everything, she circled Dad like a crow swooping on a shiny scrap. She was wearing her most tentlike dress, kelly green. A string of fake pearls hung around her fleshy neck as always. She had gotten new earrings to match her necklace—clip-ons with the pearl set in an opened, gold-plated clam. Her voice echoed through the house: "What funeral home, James? Mary, get me the Yellow Pages. I can't believe you never planned for this, James. James? I know. Shhh. C'mon. I know, dear. I know."

I found Ma's blue Valium at the back of the linen closet's top shelf and gave Colleen half a pill to stop her crying. She quieted twenty minutes after she ate the other half. After a few more paces around the house, through the kitchen, the dining room, the living room, the kitchen again, she sat back in the living room armchair to drip her quiet tears down her face and onto her blouse as she smoothed the green felt of the upholstery first one way, then the other, with her fingertips.

I kept my ear to the phone, writing down names and crossing them off on a big pad of legal paper, still in my work clothes: blue jeans, army boots, a T-shirt with a print of Picasso's *Don Quixote*, which was dabbed with jelly and confectioners' sugar. Jack sat on the other side of the kitchen table, completely still except for his eyes watching me and every other person or thing that moved. Dad and Addy made arrangements in the basement rec room. Colleen in her white, high-collared blouse and navy blue skirt slowly unraveled, quiet and damp in her armchair.

This was also the time of Roman. I'd known about him for a month, got together with him a week and a half earlier. Do you call a guy you've done it with twice but still don't know very well to tell him your mother just died? I decided: No, you don't.

Between calls to other friends, Dad came into the kitchen and said, "Did you eat yet? There's the roast your ma made Friday. We could have some of that." He held his jaw tight as a vise grip, like he'd been practicing how to talk before he came up. "Or Addy said she'd go get Kentucky Fried Chicken, if you want that instead." He sat down at the table with us, touching the stubble on the end of his chin with the tip of his thumb. "What do you think?"

"It doesn't matter, Dad," I said.

"Chicken would be good," Jack said.

"Okay then." He tapped the table with all his fingers at the same time. "Stupid, stupid, stupid!" he said, not even trying to hold back the spit on the *p*'s. "That's a God-damned stupid thing to do, driving drunk. What in hell's name is wrong with that woman?" His beautiful black eyebrows hunched together. "Just a little drink with the girls after school," he said, each word slow, deliberate. "*Teachers*." His mouth bent the word into a curse.

Dad combed his hands through the hair on each side of his head. For a second I thought he'd start pulling, but he only clasped his fingers behind his head. When he let go, he started talking again with a quiet, slow lurch toward the table and he put his hands between his knees as if to warm them. "Don't ever drive drunk. Any of you." He stared at the table, whispered through his teeth. "Only an idiot would do something that stupid." His voice took on the shape and timbre I'd only heard when he talked to Ma, his body taut, his tone savagely calm. If I didn't know better, I'd have thought Ma was in the room and they were fighting as usual.

He pushed himself off from the table, walked down to the basement. The stairs creaked under the weight and rhythm of his step, the way they do only for him: one foot louder and a fraction faster than the other, beating his rhythm on the stairs.

Mrs. Hennessey was the last call I made. I told her I wouldn't be back in to work for a week or so; she or Jess would have to open the bakery until then, because with Ma's dying, there were just so many things to do. I hung up and tried to think of something to do. Jack and I pulled on our boots and coats and gloves to help Dad shovel the walk and driveway, but he said no. He needed to be alone. Jack got out the cards to play solitaire. It was only nine o'clock, too early to go to bed, and I wasn't tired anyway. Jack's cards said flip, flip, flip to the table. I tried to feel something, or rather to figure how I felt. I felt weird, like an unshaded light bulb on the ceiling of a doctor's exam room or in a prisoner's interrogation room. Or something like that: alive, alone, emitting a low monotone hum. I asked Jack if he wanted to play crazy eights, and he said sure.

Jack would need a whole new suit. A trip to the mall was the only answer. With his dark eyes and hair black like Dad's, he was easy to dress except for his being so pale. Colleen's coloring was more like Ma's than mine with her auburn hair and brown eyes. We'd have to pick something out for her instead of bringing her with us. Black, I knew, went well with my black hair and blue eyes.

After the second game of crazy eights, Jack conked out, and it seemed like a good idea to get some sleep. I heard Addy come back in a little while later crinkling the bags of fried chicken. The deep-fried smell crept through the house, settled in as if it would stay forever. She and Dad murmured low in the kitchen, voices rising, falling, shifting like wind against a windowpane.

I lay in bed trying to sleep, struggled to conjure any kind of picture other than Ma in the car, Ma crashing, Ma after the crash. I had seen her that morning, but hadn't paid any real attention to her. I couldn't even remember what she was wearing.

* * *

Ma was the worst singer I'd ever heard, but she was a genius on guitar, piano, any instrument she touched. She and Mrs. Kraus starred at St. Benedict's twelve o'clock guitar Mass. Mrs. Kraus sang reasonably well and had ambition, so it wasn't long before they were traveling around to nursing homes, Ma switching off between piano and guitar, Mrs. Kraus tearing it up with French torch songs or American ballads.

When Mrs. Kraus moved to Arizona, the nursing home directors begged Ma to still come. The old people, who were restless and bored to begin with, became absolutely depressed when Ma showed up with only the guitar. "Just sing," one director told her. "They don't care how you sound." So she did. Although she came home crying that first day, it became a favorite story for her. The way Ma told it, there's nothing worse than a man hooked up to an oxygen tank booing you with what little breath he has left. From then on, she tried to enlist each of us kids to come with her, Jack sometimes dancing a little while Ma played, Colleen crooning "Speak Low (When You Speak Love)," me in the corner holding Mrs. Taylor's shaky sweating hand, marveling at the way her blue-green veins shone through the gray translucent skin.

Ma tried to teach all of us an instrument or two when we were young, but something in me was missing. I made sure to put my fingers in the proper places to strike the right chord, but the music never came.

"Apply yourself," Ma'd say. So I tried harder. Colleen played every instrument like she was born for it, singing in her deep, resonant voice, smiling at anyone who listened. Jack played piano and guitar, and easily slipped into a soft shoe number without fear or embarrassment. Dad, on special occasions, held up his head and sang with a voice dark and sweet as dusk. I applied myself, but all I ever got was plink, plink, plunk.

"It's okay, Mary," she said after one particularly long lesson. "You'll find something."

On the altar when Mrs. Kraus sang, Ma played without even paying attention to what she was doing with her fingers, her face turned toward Mrs. Kraus, watching her as if she were in love. Sometimes Ma's lips moved as Mrs. Kraus's voice vaulted over us, holding one note, high and clear. "Marry a man who can sing," Ma always said. "If he breaks your heart one day, he'll break it completely, and it can never happen again." She'd tip her glass to Dad when she said it, and he'd sing the lowest note on the scale, "dooooooooooooooo," prolonging it until he ran out of breath.

When Ma played alone, with no one singing,

her face filled up with a terrific wonder. I wanted whatever came to her when she played to fill me up too. A person could consume an entire life looking for that kind of wonder, as if it really were something to find just by looking for it, like a shiny penny face up on a sidewalk.

Tuesday, the morning after the accident, Jack and I struck out for Wonderland Mall. Six inches of snow had fallen. Everything looked big and clean.

"I don't like that," or "It makes you look dumpy," Jack told me of the things I tried on for him. As usual, he was right. For Colleen he would have just shaken his head a little or scrunched his eyebrows together. She couldn't stand anyone telling her no. "Does this look okay?" she'd ask Jack, and if he told her what he really thought, she'd get angry, but then she'd change into whatever Jack suggested.

We left the store without getting anything.

"I hate Wonderland," he said. "Let's just get something and go."

"Jack," I said.

"Then we should go someplace decent. There's nothing but shit here."

"It's not a fashion show."

"We should look our very best for Ma," he said.

Again, he was right. Everything here was the

same as everything else. His liveliness, his unabashed appreciation of beauty and style regardless of what was considered popular, was a quality I had just begun to learn. Even though I was older, he taught me to look hard and honestly at what appealed to me, to slough off the regard of others.

He'd gone quiet again as we walked out of the mall, and then out of the blue, he came out with, "Isn't it weird."

I looked over at him as we walked. We had all learned to wait for Jack when he was working out an idea.

"Fashion. Clothes. Everything really. Music, art, movies, books. We're all just what we take on and what we cast off. Ma was her own person. A good example."

"Eighteen going on thirty-eight." I laughed, but he didn't understand what was so funny.

We'd been in Wonderland for only an hour. By the time we left, the temperature had shot into the fifties and it was raining. The snow was more than half gone, and everything changed back to gray.

At Fairlane Mall, we picked out two dresses for Colleen. A suit for Jack, for me two dresses, a new pair of shoes, and while Jack went to get us both hot pretzels, I got an extra little something—a sexy slip in case Roman found out and called to console me.

I wasn't prepared for such diversions, my mind occupied with things totally unrelated to Ma. I found myself itching for sex, always a bit dewy. I should have been thinking about Ma, and I did occasionally, but then I tried not to, and in the meantime I couldn't stop touching myself.

Roman was the first guy who seemed to offer the possibility of more than just sex. But of course I wanted sex too. I was just entering my world. I had thought it was enough to recognize that a gulf could exist between sex and love. I had no idea yet how frightening and complicated the human touch could become, the awful disorientation involved in what it takes to be loved, or to love. How, once you get used to touching and being touched, the absence of it can drive you crazy. I didn't know what it meant to be alone. I was young and pretty. At that point, all I had to do was smile to get attention.

I had talked to Ma about sex very little, in the most general terms, and I never completely told the truth.

By the time we got home from the mall, Jack and I were laughing. The snow was melting fast, the sun came out, and the rain had stopped for good. A Herman's Hermits song played on the oldies station, and we sang along in exaggerated English accents about the *loof-lay* daughter of Mrs. Brown. We walked through the front door to see Colleen hunched over, pounding out bread dough on the kitchen table, kneading and rolling it into a big ball, scattering flour everywhere in a cloud, and still crying. Addy sat at the table picking tiny pieces off a new batch of oatmeal raisin cookies. She has devoured whole plates of food this way, bit by tiny bit, as if she didn't even realize she'd been eating.

"Jesus, Coll," Dad said when he came down from his room. He put his hand on her shoulder, but she jerked it away.

"I'm just crying," she said. "For God's sake, that's not so unusual, is it?"

Addy lifted her eyebrows at Dad, jerked her head a little as if to say: Stand back. Instead of standing back, Dad took Colleen by the shoulders and forcefully turned her around. He hugged her close to him, and although she struggled at first, he wouldn't let her go. Both their bodies shook in the middle of the kitchen.

Jack and I, in the glow of our new purchases, stood in the doorway. Jack muttered, "Oh God," and ran to his room. Addy slowly walked over, put the flat of her hand on Dad's back, took it away, then put it back again. The skin under Addy's arm shook in rhythm to Dad and Colleen's sobs. Everywhere I looked, the room blurred and cleared, blurred and cleared.

* * *

I longed to be at work instead of home. I wanted to hang out with Jess to take my mind off this mess. Jess started at the bakery the week after I did. She had dyed black the tips of her naturally blond hair, even her very short bangs. She had the best body on a short person I've ever seen. A year earlier, she had gone to London for a week or two and, once back, peppered her speech with British phrases using a fake Cockney accent. "Bollocks," she'd say. "'Oo put the bloody blintzes 'ere on the bleedin' bread board, I'd like to know."

Jess introduced me to a new bootleg club in an abandoned brick building that we called the City Club because it used to house the historic Women's City Club of Detroit. The building stood among other rutted, dilapidated buildings on a block halfway between the Cass Corridor and the Detroit River waterfront. Each floor was perfectly square, a large dark space into which music was pumped. Scattered around the old wooden floor on the third and first levels were ratty couches next to old television sets, which showed bootleg videotapes from new punk bands. You could dance wherever there was enough room, but the second floor was the best, cleared out completely except for a few bar stools around the perimeter of the room.

We had taken to going to the City Club every Wednesday and Saturday night. Jess had a crush on a bartender there who was also in her mythology class at Wayne State. On the night I met Roman, Jess was dressed all in white: white miniskirt, low white leather boots, white T-shirt.

"Smashing," I told her. I wore faded, peg-legged jeans, blue suede boots, and an undershirt of Dad's I'd dyed bright orange, cut off the collar, and wore off one shoulder.

Ivan, the bartender, told her to come early so he could show her around and introduce her to the DJ. Ivan had swoopy dark hair and a muscular face like Bryan Ferry. We arrived at 9 p.m., before anybody else. I heard The Jam's song, "Start!" playing on the second floor, then suddenly it stopped in the middle of the song. Ivan took us to meet Roman, who was spinning. Our footsteps rang up from the wooden floor, bounced off the walls, and came back to us full force, as did our voices. Midway across the floor, the music came on again for half a second, then off again.

"Roman jams on the echo," Ivan told us. "He plays with it a little in the first few numbers, before the crowd comes and the bodies absorb the sound."

Ivan led us to a hut at the back of the room. Here Roman sat on the floor surrounded by six red milk crates full of record albums. He looked up.

"Hi," Roman said before anyone spoke. He met each of our eyes and nodded.

It looked as though he'd shaved his head a week or two earlier. The stubble was just beginning to prickle through his scalp again, and his ears stuck out dramatically. His eyes were huge and brown, calm as a full moon. The army green T-shirt he wore was a little too small for him. It said CLASH in red block letters.

"More reverb?" Roman asked Ivan.

"Reverb keeps it alive." They said it simultaneously and laughed. There was a sign tacked against the wall above Roman's head that said the same thing painted in dark green paint on a thin piece of plywood.

"Once a sound happens," Roman said to Jess and me, "it goes away immediately. Reverb keeps it alive," and this time he didn't laugh. "I'm Roman," he said as he stood up. He shook Jess's hand first, then mine as Ivan introduced us.

The second floor filled with people within an hour. It was winter. The movement and the cigarette smoke heated the place up quickly. I sat on the second-floor window ledge to get some air, one leg inside with my foot on the wood floor, one leg hanging out high above the broken concrete below. I had a good view of the door where I could watch people enter and leave: mohawks and skinheads and style mongers of all sorts wafting in and out and up and down the stairs to the third and first floors—flitting, floating, flirting.

Later that night, Roman emerged from his back room hut, walked quickly across the dance floor, and said, "Come with me." He led me to the back room and let me pick out the music. The first song I picked was the Sex Pistol's "Sub-Mission," and the rest of the night was mine.

A week later I went to a party at Roman's house with Jess. Roman's parents had gone to Toronto for the weekend. His friends spoke English and Ukrainian, switching randomly between the two all evening. Ivan ignored Jess. She was pissed, but told me Ivan could go fuck himself, then she stood still, sighed deeply, scanned the room with her head tilted to one side as if she were examining a painting in a museum, and within five minutes three different guys walked over to introduce themselves. Later on, when Roman's friend George had offered her a ride home, I said that maybe I should go too, since I had driven.

"That's okay," said Jess. "I want to go with George."

Roman said, "Don't go." He squeezed my hand when I shrugged, and he said it again. "Don't go." It was cold on his porch saying goodbye to his friends. We stood without touching, but close enough that his arm gave off heat like a radiator. As the last people left, we watched their taillights glow, then fade, blink, and finally disappear before we walked back into the house, together.

He was the first guy with whom I felt a glimmer of "I could get used to this." For the time being, I convinced myself, he'd be fine to keep around.

Those days. My mother—a woman brimming with fault and beauty—dies, and I think about some guy, my prurient interests, the spreading heat and light of lust. Ma's charm lay in her strange mixture of coarseness and grace. I have never been like her. She was a woman capable of keeping people around. Here I am so many years later, and between Pilates and martinis and watching another friend die from one of the ever-lengthening list of plagues visited upon my family and friends over the years—AIDS, cancer, overdoses, suicides—why do I covet those days?

There are lots of things I have never become: a nurse, a mother, faithful.

When I think of Roman now, I see he was just another skinny guy with brown eyes. He could have been anybody. I have picked out boyfriends with less discrimination than I pick out a new pair of shoes, and have worn them out far sooner.

By six o'clock Wednesday, the house filled with food. Between Colleen's constant baking and the neighbors with their ceramic dishes and Tupperware filled with potato salad, meat loaf, roasts, hams, casseroles, and such, there were plates piled high on all shelves of the refrigerator, and covering most of the countertops in the kitchen.

Jack stayed in the living room, ready to greet the next batch of visitors in order to keep Colleen focused and engaged in the kitchen. That's when Roman called to ask me out again. He sounded happy, and I realized he hadn't heard about Ma. Just after I got on the phone, he said, "Hold on," and I heard him say something to one of his parents in Ukrainian. The language itself seems so harsh with its hard consonants and diphthongs, but when he spoke, I heard the soft vowels, his voice delicate, almost feminine, and suddenly all I could think of was his penis. The head was completely round, like the head of an exotic fish, the skin so soft and just a little darker than the rest of his body. His was the first uncircumcised penis I'd ever seen. I loved watching the skin move under the rhythm of my hand.

"So what're you doing tonight?" he said when he came back on the phone.

"Roman," I said. "I was going to call you."

"Yeah?" he said. "What were you going to call me? Something good, I hope."

"No," I said. "My mother died." It was so strange that I let out a little laugh.

"Really?" he said, and he laughed too.

"Yes," I said. "Really." I couldn't think of anything else to say. "Listen, I have to go," I said. "Sorry this was . . . I know this was . . . awkward. Sorry."

"Mary, I'm . . ." he began, and I hung up.

Dad walked downstairs from his and Ma's bedroom, both thumbs supporting hangers with dresses. Colleen stopped cooking to look at him.

Dad said, "Mary?"

Jack walked into the kitchen and looked cautiously at Colleen, who stood, spoon in hand dripping chocolate frosting down her wrist and onto the kitchen floor.

"Even though it'll have to be closed," Dad said. "The casket. I thought . . ."

Jack took the hangers away from Dad, threw four of the dresses on the couch, and showed me the other two: a simply cut, deep purple dress and a fancier black-and-white thing I'd never liked on her. I pointed to the purple. Jack collected the other five and took Dad and the hangers with dresses back upstairs.

Everything was arranged. The wake on Thursday, the funeral Friday morning, all our clothes. And again we entered a lull, all of us home, food everywhere as if it were a holiday. There was no way to be alone, and it was getting on my nerves.

I finally said, "Okay, Colleen. That's enough.

You're not making any more food. I'll help you clean up." I took a large mixing bowl from a counter and began collecting dirty utensils and smaller appliances in it. "The dishwasher's full. We'll do these by hand. I'll wash. You dry."

Somewhere between the blender blades and a large metal pot, Colleen said, "Point three blood alcohol. That's high, huh?"

I was in tenth grade before I had noticed that Ma drank more than a bottle of wine every day by herself. One day when Jack had the flu and Dad was working overtime again, I took out the week's trash. It dawned on me in the midst of dragging the rattling, clinking garbage bags to the curb that those weren't pop bottles in there, since we returned those for the ten-cent deposit. Halfway down the driveway, I opened up one bag to count eleven empty wine bottles.

"What do you think?" I said, trying to sound kind, trying to sound as if it were just occurring to me too.

"It's not like she was an alcoholic," Colleen said, her voice firm and final.

The water was gray, and the suds had coalesced into a scummy film.

"A lot of people drink," she said. "Most people. It's nice." She concentrated on drying a glass. "It's easy to get carried away."

I let out the drain, loaded a new batch of dishes into the sink, then filled up the sink again, pouring in dishwashing liquid until we couldn't see anything distinctly under the suds.

She said, "It's like when you play music, or sing, you know?"

"No," I said. "I don't."

The sounds of water and soap swishing around in the sink took over the room.

"A lot of things are like that," she said. "Intoxicating. You're full, then when it's over, you're empty, maybe more empty than when you began." She snapped her towel, found a dry spot, wiped down a spatula. "The urge always comes back." She set the spatula carefully in the drawer, leaned her hip against the counter to rest, waiting for me. "It's like there's never enough of anything, you know?"

"Yeah," I said. I had no idea what she was talking about, but she had stopped crying. I wondered if she'd helped herself to more of Ma's Valium. I finished washing a big ceramic bowl and handed it to her carefully so it wouldn't slip and break.

"He kissed me on our first date," Ma had told me. "In the salt mine. He was as wiry then as he is now, just like Jack."

We were in the dressing room at Hudson's, and

she was trying on a new dress. I was eighteen. She was supposed to be helping me pick out a dress for my high school graduation and had decided she needed something new for herself. I leaned against the dressing room wall, watched her pull on a sleeveless baby blue wool dress. I squinched up my nose. Not her best color.

"I wish I could wear blue," she sighed. "Are you nervous?"

"Not especially," I said. "You met Dad at a party, right?"

"I was catering it. Bartender, cook, waitress, everything. I can't remember why he was there, who he knew. Oh, yes, I do. It was that blowhard friend of his, Bill Flanagan. What a puke. Wanted to show the world how *suave* he was, having a party catered. I was just trying to make a little money. I didn't know a damned thing about catering, but Flanagan's mother knew mine, and that I liked to cook, and—voilà!—Hannah, the caterer." She made a deep bow before turning around to let me unzip her. I stood behind her and we looked at each other in the mirror while she talked. "And he asked me out when I handed him his margarita. He sipped it over the salted rim, licked his lips, and said, 'Ever been to the salt mine?' So we went."

She let the dress crumple around her ankles,

bending a little when she stepped out of it. I watched the soft folds of her belly wrinkle together, her stretch marks visible in the lax skin until she straightened up again. The skin of her torso pulled back smooth and taut enough to hide the fact that she'd borne three children.

"He seemed so quiet, so mysterious. Ha! He was a hard nut to crack, your father." She turned and leaned back against the mirror. "Do you know what I remember most about it?" She looked like she was going to laugh, head bent slightly, hair hooked behind her left ear with a finger. With her face turned full to me, coupled with the image of her profile in the mirror, it was easy to see how Dad was beguiled.

"There was an echo in the mine. We were on some awful tour with a bunch of other people, and we hung back in one of the caverns. 'Look at this,' he said. He took hold of my finger and ran it against one of the walls. Then he licked it. My finger, not the wall. Then he kissed me. Our lips made a little smack when we separated. We both heard it; the kiss and the echo." She had taken hold of my finger and run it across the cool mirror to illustrate. I felt my fingertip more than I was ever aware of feeling it in my life, and for a longer time than I expected.

"Amazing," she said, and then pulled her jeans and shirt back on. Before we walked out of the dressing room, she took me by the arm. "Mary," she said. "Promise you'll tell me when all this starts for you."

"I will," I lied.

During the wake on Thursday, Dad held up pretty well. It was almost a comfort to have Colleen blubbering away, because it gave us something to do, getting her Kleenex, rubbing her back, bringing her water.

People roamed in and out. I kept imagining all the men naked, wondering if they thought of me naked too.

Colleen wouldn't let Aunt Addy put Ma's guitar on the casket. She took hold of the guitar with her fingers so tight around it, I thought it might snap in two.

"She wasn't your mother or your wife, Aunt Addy," Colleen said. "Why do we have to put anything on the casket?"

"I've never been to a closed casket wake where there was nothing on the casket," Addy whispered. "To remind everyone what she was like. To distract, if nothing else. We can't very well put a wineglass up there, now can we?"

Dad's shoulders, chest, and chin shifted toward the center of his body.

When Addy saw her remark hit Dad more than

Colleen, she made a grab for his arm. "Oh, James," she said, "I didn't mean it." And to Colleen, "Do you see what this is doing to your father?"

"God damn you," Colleen said, but Dad interrupted her with a simple "Please."

He straightened his shoulders, put up one hand, and left. For three hours we told anyone who asked that Dad would be back any minute. When he finally came back, he put their wedding picture on the casket and sat down with me. He had taken off his suit coat, rolled up his sleeves, and with his fingers combed the dark hairs on his arms so they all fell in the same direction. "I started rummaging through old pictures," he said, "and I fell asleep. Oh, Mary." He lifted his head and looked out over the room. "That's horrible, isn't it?" he said. He looked back down at the floor. "Christ."

"Everyone understands," I told him. "It's good you took a rest."

"Do you know how long it's been since I've slept alone?" he asked me. Only now, after year upon year of tangling myself in the ecstatic limbs of man after ever-new man, do I understand the depth of sadness in my father's question that day. But at the time his vulnerability frightened me, so I left it alone. I kept my mouth shut, patted his back to quiet him.

* * *

Other than Colleen's pink swollen eyes, we all looked neat and poised on the morning of the funeral. The church was decorated for Lent, and suddenly I was very happy about having chosen the purple dress for Ma, even if nobody would ever see it, because purple is for Passion.

Beyond that, my memory fails me. I kept trying to figure out what was missing, until the rhythms of the Mass overtook me. Prayers were just words, and words were only sounds rising and falling with no meaning beyond the surprising surge that comes from hearing something forgotten become familiar again. I don't remember the eulogy, who said it, or what was said. I don't remember the saints invoked, what Father Walsh said to comfort us, or to try to comfort us, or to admit there was no comfort for us or for anyone else, ever. I don't remember who the altar boys were, or even who the pallbearers were. I don't remember if there was a smell of flowers, or of incense, the way the day shone or didn't shine through the stained glass. We sat in the front pew, so I don't even really know who else was there.

This is what I remember: Music. The rising pitch of the organ, the absence of the guitar, the upswelling surge of voices coming out of all the people we knew, combined into one strange and familiar strain of song.

Jack barely mouthed the words. He stood next to Colleen, who didn't sing at all. They were both on my left. The only voice that was distinct and recognizable was Dad's on my right. He used to sing to us when we were very little, so long ago that I had forgotten he'd stopped. I hadn't heard him sing so clear, so strong since I was a little girl. My father singing was all verb, the tone of it, its vibration, rising above all the others, alone. It wasn't so much the beauty of the note that pierced me, it was his holding of it, its singular height. His voice was strong, capable of anything, cutting through air, space, and time, slicing present from past and future, all confusion and blind fury, as if they were his only possessions. *If he keeps that up*, I thought, *he'll explode or tear the church apart.* I would like to say the columns began to crack and we were all crushed and buried under the weight of my father's exquisite grief, his horror, our own realizations of the fact that he would never touch her body, that she would never hear him sing again. But this is what really happened: The song ended, and we were left standing, altered only by the slight, invisible passage of time and our own imaginations, ready to face the rest of the day.

It was the last song. The sky outside was mottled, bruised with early spring clouds. We filed out of church holding hands, settled in with each other, and followed the black car.

* * *

Even after it had gotten dark outside, the house was still filled with people. Dad told everybody to come over after the funeral, so that none of us would have to be alone with each other. Neighbors, coworkers, people from school, old friends: They all crowded into the kitchen and living room.

I handed Jess, George, and Roman each a plate and elbowed a path to the table, where Dad stood pouring drinks for his friends, and sweating. Colleen sat at the table watching people eat, but not saying much. It had been some time since she'd cried. Jack was cornered by neighbor ladies fawning all over him, telling him stories of how they remembered when he was born, when he broke his arm falling off a fence, when Ma dressed him up as Humpty Dumpty for Halloween one year, Snoopy the next.

Aunt Addy sat in her usual spot at the table picking at food.

"Who's your young man, Mary?" she said.

Colleen said with almost no energy at all, "Shut up, Aunt Addy."

"Colleen, your hair is so pretty like that," Aunt Addy said, taking the opportunity to stroke it lightly. "You look very much like your mother with it that way."

"Thank you," Colleen said. She slowly leaned

away from Addy's hand, keeping both arms crossed over her chest, and repeated, "Shut up and leave Mary alone."

"Yes," Addy said, "just like your mother." She found an empty plate and forked a small dab of potato salad onto it. "This looks good," she said.

Jess and George didn't stay long. Roman and I walked them to the car. It was still cold, but because I didn't want to go back inside, Roman and I went for a walk around the block. I put on the black motorcycle jacket I had bought at a secondhand store the week before. He made me stand still while he zipped it up for me, like I was a little kid. He pulled on a black wool cap to cover his head. It made him look like a cat burglar or some kind of thug. A cute thug.

"Is this weird for you?" I asked him.

"No," he said. "No. Not at all." He paused. "Well, yeah, I mean, of course, but you know." We walked for a long time without saying anything, which I realized wasn't too unusual, given that we really didn't know each other at all. I was going to tell him thanks for coming and see you later. There would be other guys. I was going to tell him soon.

"So, how are you?" he said. I don't know what came over me, but I started laughing and could not stop. The more I laughed, the giddier I became, until I was laughing so hard, I could barely breathe. Minutes passed before I could see Roman clearly, and I could tell I had frightened him, which made me laugh even harder.

"Maybe we should walk toward home," he said, taking hold of my elbow, but instead I sat down on the curb at the corner to catch my breath. With the temperature yo-yoing up and down over the past few days, everything was dry, but very cold again. The streetlight hummed low and steady above our heads. The night was clear. After a while I settled down to a slow giggle, then the hiccups began, loud, indelicate, bouncing off into the night.

"Oh. I'm so sorry," I said between hiccups. "You must think I'm a freak." That's when Roman kissed me, long, slow, hard, until I hiccupped in the middle of it and we both started laughing.

"I think you're right," I said. "We should head back." We walked past his car. A couple minutes more wouldn't hurt, I thought. Fewer shapes and shadows moved past the fogged kitchen windows, but there were still quite a few people inside, so I guided Roman to the backyard. Our family kept the picnic table up all year long, and when Roman and I sat down on it, I said, "My hiccups stopped."

I was free to take him or leave him. A whole void of freedom opened up for me. It's odd to take a moment from so long ago and fill it with all the things

I didn't know then: that Ma was the brave one, who cultivated the wisdom and courage love requires; that it would be as difficult for me to learn to risk love as it was for me to learn music, and that despite what I thought I wanted, it would become easier to let go of love than to work to hold on to it. How could I know that Jack, the only one as brave as Ma, would unfreeze and bloom, capping off his first few freewheeling years by falling in love with Diego, who even Dad would come to love? That falling in love wouldn't save him or Diego, and that we'd all watch helplessly as they both withered thin as whispers, two of the first to disappear in the plague? That Colleen would feed her bitterness until it grew out of all proportion along with her own flesh? That once Ma was gone, Dad's drifting away from us was as natural as his gradual return to us a year later? That the happiness we had in those years of Mom and Dad in love could only be lived once?

Back then I only knew what most girls that age know. I was alive, all in working order, my palms open, my heart still hammering in exquisite repetition: clenching, unclenching, and clenching again.

I kissed Roman over and over. I didn't know if I would see him again, but right then all I wanted was him inside me and the sky with its stars above us faint and far away. I touched the outside of his pants, but he pushed my hand away saying no, it didn't seem right, but then kissed me all the harder, biting my lips gently, gently, and again.

I straddled him, my legs under the table, his stretched out over the dead winter grass, and he kissed my neck, pulled my hair, tilting back my head, and kissed my throat. Clear night sky. I felt him move under me. My underwear came off with a little effort, and I settled back onto his lap. Chipped paint on the wood of the picnic table scraped the tops of my thighs and the backs of my calves. One of the bench boards was loose, giving as we rocked. A rip, and the crinkle of the cellophane package sent a shiver up my spine and back again, and we maneuvered together, my flat palms crawling over the rough tabletop. The zipper on my jacket sounded like electricity as he pulled it down.

He kissed me, his hand on the back of my head, tugging at my hair again, tilting my head back up to the sky and kissing his way as far down as he could. The stars glittered like fireflies dangling over a dark lake, tiny spots of light that I knew had to be moving at enormous speeds between unfathomable distances. People used to believe that the movements of planets in the deep spaces between the stars created music: the harmony of the spheres, they called it. I wanted to pretend I heard that music, but all I could hear was my own voice saying, "Yes." I whispered it above his head into the dark. "Right there," I said. "Oh . . ." I said, but suddenly I couldn't remember his name. I clutched him close to me as tightly as possible.

"Fill me up," I said, my voice low, desperate, whispering, afraid someone might hear me.

Crystalline

Hannah and Addy were at it again, and as usual, James was right in the middle.

"If I hear 'He's my brother' one more time . . . She doesn't control this house." Hannah stopped to dig something out of her tooth with her tongue. "And you just sit there."

James's large nose disappeared into the mug when he tipped it to sip his coffee. His brown eyes over the rim fixed calmly on his wife. Hannah, as if knowing this was as much of a response as she'd get, added, "It's not my fault she has no one else."

James set down his mug and cocked his head to chide Hannah. "It's a month away," he said. "An old man's birthday."

"Forty-seven isn't old. And you're my husband. And Mary and Colleen and Jack's father." She broke sections of garlic off the clove, scooped the skins off the table into her palm, and clapped her hands over the trash bin.

"And Addy's brother," James added. He pressed

his lips together and squinched his mouth so she had no other choice but to laugh. He liked making her laugh. She unleashed one of her long groans that started as a high, off-pitch note and slowly descended to a growlish purr.

"I don't even want a party," James said.

"Well, why didn't you say that?"

"I *keep* saying it."

Hannah turned her back to him. "It should be just us." She pulled out the first bottle of wine and poured herself a glass. "Our own little party, here. No organizing necessary." She pulled out the second bottle and set it aside so it would be handy when dinner was ready. "She doesn't cook, but she has to be in control. So now we have to go to a restaurant for your birthday."

"See?" James said. "I say *no* party, you say *our* party."

"Well, you don't mean it."

"And Addy can cook."

"Cook. What? Cookies? Cake?" Hannah said. She held a tomato captive on the cutting board with her left hand, paused over it with the knife in her right hand, and gave James her "significant look" before quickly dispatching the tomato.

She'd just taken her after-work shower. The copper and silver in her hair took on more complex and beautiful colors when wet. She wore jeans and a V-neck sweater without a bra underneath. She still looked mighty fine. James watched the twitch in her thin shoulders as she chopped celery, and followed the curve of her back down to her hips. He loved the feel of her hip bone under his hand when he reached from behind, and he hoped she wouldn't be too tired or too drunk later.

Nothing about this moment was different from so many other moments in their married life, but James would find himself over the years coming back to it repeatedly. This was Detroit, 1980. He didn't know at this point that on the upcoming Monday his wife would spin out the end of her days in a car, on a patch of ice, with a blood alcohol level that steamed above three times the legal limit. Darkness, a skidding car, a cyclone fence, and a very large tree would soon erase everything James had once thought permanent and sure. But he didn't know that yet. So after Hannah's groan, as she poured her second glass and said sarcastically, "Family," James simply shook his head, sighed, and said, "Yeah. Family."

"It's all set," Addy said. "Mario's."

James had spent all Saturday avoiding Addy. He purposely didn't call, and hoped she wouldn't drop by, but on Saturday night she called to give him a chore, so here he was Sunday on one knee braiding together different colored wires, clipping off their plastic coatings, and splaying out the copper strands before twisting together the right ones and capping them. Addy was on a splurge. She'd been given a raise and a promotion to office manager at the doctor's office. The television that James was now hooking up for her was her first big buy, and the birthday celebration she'd planned for James at Mario's Fine Dining was her second.

"They still have that big back private room, but we'd need at least twelve for that. There'll only be the six of us, so we'll have to eat out front with all the other people."

James's knee cracked when he stood. He turned on the set and stood back. The screen bloomed from a pinpoint of light to a commercial with a chaos of orange, pink, and yellow lights reflecting off the silvery sparkles on the costumes. *Dance Fever* was coming on at six thirty, and Nipsey Russell was going to be a guest.

"Oh," said Addy. She sat on the couch and adjusted her floral house dress to billow over the shelves of her flesh. She stared at the screen, transfixed. James flipped the knob through the channels, adjusting the rabbit ears to get a better picture.

"How's that?" he asked.

"Great. Oh, it's just great. Thank you, James. You wouldn't believe it. I was going crazy after the old one died. I got home from eight o'clock Mass this morning, and didn't even have the television to keep me company." She looked at the screen, smiling, and sank farther into the couch cushions. "Oh, that's grand."

The picture changed to President Carter, then to Ronald Reagan saying something behind a podium, and James turned off the set. Addy blinked a few times.

"Can you take the old one out to the dumpster for me? I can help carry it."

He removed some papers from the old television and put them on top of the new set.

"Oh, that's what I wanted to show you," Addy said. "I got menus from Mario's, so they can look them over. It's still early, but if we had to, I suppose we could change."

"Listen, Addy, I was thinking. Maybe it'd be best if we just all ate at home. At our house."

"But you love Mario's. We used to go there all the time for our birthdays. Remember?"

James pushed the rolling TV table back into place and pulled on his jacket.

"Oh. I see," said Addy. "It's her. She doesn't want

to go. Fine. I'll change the reservation to five people instead of six."

"Adelaide."

"I should be able to do something special for my brother on his birthday. I'm tired of her ruining all our plans. If she doesn't like it, she doesn't have to come."

"Well, you know that's not going to happen."

"If she's worried about the drinking, you can tell her I can afford a couple of bottles of wine."

She saw his irritation at her bringing it up again.

"Well, I'm sorry, James, but you know it's true. That's probably why she's so skinny."

James laughed. "Come on, Addy."

"It's a medical fact, James," she said louder and more forcefully. "Big drinkers don't eat right. They barely eat at all. All their calories come from the booze."

"Hannah has never been fat. She was thin even when she was pregnant."

"There was that year after she had Jack . . ."

"That was different. He was our third kid, and she had some trouble after that."

"Hmmpph. There was trouble, all right," she said barely under her breath.

"That's our business, Addy, and it was a long time

ago. Jack'll be graduating from high school in June. Jesus. Can you believe that?"

"I'm not canceling the reservation. She can come or not, but we're having your birthday at Mario's just like we used to do before she came along. I knew there'd be trouble, that's why I booked it so early."

"We'll all be there, Addy. I'll handle it. But please don't stir the pot in the meantime. There's no need to bring it up again. To Hannah or the kids. Okay?"

Addy didn't answer. She liked rubbing it in even more than she liked winning, so James was hollowing out her victory.

"I'd rather spend my birthday alone than go through this shit every year."

Addy glanced at her watch. "Oh! *Bill Kennedy* is on in a minute. Do you want to stay and watch with me?"

"I should get home."

Addy moved to the kitchen. "It's a good one. Cary Grant. *Arsenic and Old Lace*."

James shook his head.

"You sure? I made a bundt cake." She lifted a plate that held a cake dripping white glaze down its sides and placed it on the table in front of the television. "Let me see if Channel 50 comes in before you leave."

She turned the television back on and changed

the channel. The picture was somewhat blurry, but cleared up after fiddling a little with the rabbit ears.

James zipped up, flicked his head toward the door before picking up the old television. "Can you get the door?"

When James was halfway to the dumpster, which was at the end of the row of apartments, Addy leaned out with one foot on the welcome mat and said loudly to James's back, "Tell her she's got a month to get used to it. It'll be very nice."

It was very cold. She stood at her opened door until James had tipped the old TV into the dumpster and gotten into his car. He beeped twice and drove away.

In the fifties, when they were young, Mario's was hopping. There were small clubs all over, on the west side, downtown by the university, and on the east side by the river with live music, usually jazz singers or rock and roll, depending on the club.

James had left the farm in Bad Axe, coming down to live with Addy in Detroit after their parents died in what seemed to James quick succession: their mother of the flu when Addy was eighteen and James fifteen; their father three years later after getting kicked in the head by a feverish mare. They sold the farm, which had never done well anyway, and James worked for a time as a handy man in a garage on Detroit's east side, then used some of the money from the farm to pay for an electrician's course. Addy had come down years earlier to work in the office of one of the older siblings from a neighboring farm who had become a dentist. Having no other friends at first, he and Addy painted the town when they could. Everybody ate at Mario's before going out later to the clubs. Men in their skinny ties and pointy shoes would strut through escorting girls in colorful outfits with unnaturally long eyelashes and hair piled high. James loved it. Most of his wages went for rent and clothes. In the jazz clubs he wore a suit, a tie, and a good hat, but if they went to see someone like Buddy Holly at the Fox, it was more relaxed. James found that even if he just wore jeans and a good shirt, he could still look good, as long as his shoes were cool. Addy had to try a little harder and didn't always hit the mark. Since they went out together, everyone assumed they were a couple. They became regulars at the clubs, and James, who made friends easily, made a point of expanding their circle to increase the possibility of finding someone to date for both him and for Addy.

Addy went on a few dates, but none of the men were good enough for her. James went on a lot of dates and had a lot of fun, but something held him back from these women. They were pleasant and pretty and often funny, but all of them had an aura of yearning that put him off. He got the feeling that these girls, like Addy, were actively looking for someone to fit an idea in their heads. Behind everything they did, every amusement, were questions: *Will he provide? Is he good enough for me?* And they held themselves back as a result. They presented the rehearsed parts of themselves, and no matter how much fun they were having, they never entered fully into it. Eyes are just tissue surrounded by bone and skin. What was it about the eyes that told him so often something was off? The girls always said, *This was fun*, but even though he wanted to, James didn't believe them.

Hannah was different. The day of their first date was very strange. They went on a tour of the Detroit Salt Mine. It was winter, very bright, a Saturday, almost noon. He'd just picked her up, and as they were walking to the car, she touched his arm. "Look," she'd said," the moon," and pointed to the sliver of moon like a pale cut in the fabric of the western sky. The thrill he always felt at seeing the moon in broad daylight was a private joy that almost embarrassed him. When Addy still lived on the farm, James had once pointed it out to her. She responded with a snort and said, "So? What, you've never seen that before?"She shook her head at his childishness. Hannah's pointing it out brought back all his boyish joy in a rush. She put her arm across his back, her hand on his shoulder, squeezed, and released. It was like a hug, but not quite. For the first time that he could remember, he didn't want to be anywhere else but right here, right now, with her. He watched this feeling all afternoon, thinking it would pass, but it persisted. The drive to the mine, putting on the ridiculous orange hard hats, listening to the tour guide with the sleepy eye—every time he became aware of being in a moment with Hannah, he knew it was the moment he wanted to be in.

At one point, the group advanced into another chamber of the cave. He'd pinched the fabric of her coat sleeve between forefinger and thumb as a little tease to hold her back, just to see what would happen, and since they were at the back of the group anyway, it was easy. She turned with a quizzical look at him and stopped walking. The rest of the group went ahead into the next chamber.

That first kiss: salt dust and the sound. He hadn't wanted to let go. When she finally released from the kiss, her top lip separating from his two lips made a sucking smack that bounced back to them off the cave walls. Embarrassed, they laughed, and the blinky-eyed guide suddenly reappeared to scold them for not staying with the group.

When they emerged from the cave, the day was

blinding, and Hannah was almost sick with it. They had to sit in the car with the windows rolled down so she could breathe and get used to the light. By the end of it, they sat cuddled together on the front seat, his arm around her, her head on his shoulder. He always suspected she'd overplayed the headachy wooziness. By then it was five o'clock. The sliver of moon had moved in the sky, but it had also grown brighter. And this time he pointed it out to her. They kissed again, and some more.

When he drove her home, she turned to James like someone who, a little languid, a little tired, suddenly gets a second wind.

"I loved today," she said. "I can't remember when I've had so much fun."

She had folded one leg up onto the car seat so she could face him more comfortably, and once she'd said what she was thinking, she returned both feet to the floor of the car and faced the windshield.

"But," she said, "I can't figure out if it was because of the cave, or because it was with you."

"Well," he said, "of course it was because of me."

They both laughed, and she said, "I know! It was."

"No," he said. "Seriously. It's us together." But this sounded so corny, he wanted to clarify. "It's like salt. Sodium and chloride. Apart, they're not much. But together? Delicious."

It didn't come out sounding romantic the way he'd meant it, but it served as the truest reflection of what he felt.

"Oh my God," she said. "That's the dumbest thing I've ever heard." And she laughed and laughed and laughed.

Her remark shocked him, and he was hurt, but it was the moment he would point to later whenever anyone asked him when he first knew he was in love. Later, it was their code for sex, as in, *Feeling salty?* Or, *Let's get salty*.

James should have predicted that Addy would think Hannah not good enough. Addy had a habit of saying to James, whenever she felt he'd fallen short of expectations, or to spur him on to what she knew would be greatness, "Remember: We're Fallons." Clearly it meant something grand to Addy, but to James's mind, the Fallon family was a line of drifting peasants and failed farmers. They could have been tinkers in Ireland for all James knew; the lowest of the land. Addy had done some research that suggested their family had a history in Ireland as "fierce protectors."

"But we're not Irish, Addy. We're American," he once said to her, which made her furious. Their ancestors on both sides had come from Ireland, but the last two generations were born in Michigan. He thought the only reason Addy didn't try harder to break him up with Hannah was because Hannah's parents were both born in Ireland. Still, Addy had gone from being a receptionist at a dentist's office to being a receptionist at a doctor's office, and James was an electrician. He never knew what sort of greatness she was anticipating.

In their talks about dating, it was only James who expressed loneliness. Addy didn't seem to understand. "We have each other," she'd say to soothe him, and she never seemed bothered. She had boyfriends for short periods, but it seemed to James she kept these men more for show and out of a sense of duty than because of any desire to be with them. One man, Paul, even proposed to her after James and Hannah married. Addy saw Paul only on Tuesdays and Saturdays. He wanted to see her more, but according to Addy, she had to have her "own time," to do what, James never knew. And despite the fact that she grew heavier and heavier, Paul still stuck around until, after about five years, he finally gave up on Addy. Within a year of their breakup, Paul had married a woman who, although sharp-featured and not terribly pretty, was young and thin and later became a very wealthy lawyer. All Addy would ever say about it was, "What a way to make money off of people: divorce." She'd shake her head and break off another tiny piece of one of the large peanut butter cookies studded with M&M's that she always made. And after the whole cookie was gone, she'd make her old joke. "How about that?" she'd say. "I was just going to have a corner of it, but what could I do? It was round!"

"Did you handle it?" Hannah asked when James returned from Addy's. She was pounding out chicken breasts on the counter with a tenderizing mallet.

"I did." It was easier to lie to her when the wine bottle was at least half empty, as it was now. It was a small lie, meant only to keep the peace for the next month. He planned to tell Hannah a few days before his birthday and deal with it then. These are the kinds of lies allowed in a marriage. You pretend to be interested in a story you've heard her tell dozens of times before; you say it doesn't matter that she fell down drunk at the work Christmas party; and you say, "I handled it," to keep the peace for a month. Larger lies—or not lies, but silences, rather—are often better left alone. So when Hannah, for about six months after Jack was born, went "missing" from their marriage—crying jags, no sex, twenty extra pounds that wouldn't go away—and then suddenly returned to James with an alarmingly ardent embrace, he thought it wise not to ask questions that might reap answers he didn't want to hear. It rankled him that

Addy had brought up the business about the year after Jack was born. When the time came, he simply asked Hannah if everything was okay with their marriage and she threw her arms around him and said, "I love you," with such desperate force that he had no doubts after that. A little lie about a dinner a month away was certainly allowed.

"I handled it."

"Are you kidding?" Hannah said. "Really?"

He smiled.

"Ohhh." She put down the mallet, walked over to James, hooked her fingers through his belt loops, and pulled him close for a kiss. Her hair wasn't as long as when they first met, but it was still thick and healthy. Her bangs were almost long enough to sling behind her ear, and when she pulled her copper hair up and back, a wide shock of silver stood out at her left temple. He blew gently on her bangs and kissed her forehead.

"I thought you said hamburgers tonight," he said, nodding toward the chicken.

"That's for tomorrow. It has to marinate."

"No more roast beef from last night?"

"We'll have that one night during the week so I don't have to cook after work."

"A nice, peaceful birthday, that's all I want. Can

you promise me that? If Addy brings it up again, just change the subject."

"I'll make a jar of cookies as reinforcements to distract her. And brownies. And a cherry pie, just in case."

James kissed her forehead and went to fix the drip in the upstairs bathroom faucet outside their bedroom. Its constant *drip, drip, drip* had kept him awake for a week.

At six o'clock, Addy's car pulled into the driveway.

"Ma," said Jack, who was playing solitaire on the kitchen table.

"Shite," said Hannah. "I need a Valium."

Mary pulled down an extra plate from the cupboard and shooed Jack away from the table. A very wide green leather belt cinched the waist of Mary's collared white shirt, the tails of which nicely accentuated her hips. Her snug, faded peg-legged jeans were tucked into flat-heeled purple leather boots. She'd tied her long black hair into a loose bun atop her head held together with colorful pixie sticks; fetching wisps of hair fell down casually around her face. From her right ear hung an earring made of what looked like a blue jay feather.

Mary, leaning to look out the window to watch Addy get out of the car, said, "Nice outfit."

Addy had on a Sunday ensemble: a navy blue dress with white buttons, white cuffs, a white collar, white piping along the side and the hem, and navy-and-white patent leather shoes. Her earrings were large, round clip-ons, also white with a navy border. She had curled and sprayed her hair, and rouged her cheeks.

"Yuck," said Colleen. She did a brutally accurate imitation of the teeth baring and mouth stretching that accompanied Addy's constant adjustment of the bridge in her teeth. Mary and Jack laughed.

"Hey," warned Hannah. "She lives alone. Her habits are . . . different from other people's."

Colleen said, "If she doesn't like your cooking, why does she always show up at dinnertime?"

"Shh," said Hannah. "Just try to be nice to her, Colleen."

Addy's kiss left a large swath of saliva on the cheek of each of her brother's children. She stopped by, she said, because she'd just bought a new wrench, and she wanted to know if it was the right *kind* of wrench. She was going to change her shower head.

"You know how to do that?" Hannah asked.

"I'm not helpless. It comes with directions."

"Why don't you ask your super to do it?"

"He's an imbecile. I wouldn't ask him to do anything. It takes all his concentration just to screw in a light bulb. He barely has the sense to wipe his own nose."

"If you want, I can come over this week to do it," James said.

"James," said Addy. "You don't have to do that."

When James didn't insist or offer again, she said, "It can wait until next weekend. The man at the hardware store said this was one of the finest wrenches available." She thrust out her chest and imitated a hardware store man's voice. "Top of the line." She paused before continuing in her own voice. "If you decide you *want* to come over—but you don't have to—if you did, then I'd give you the wrench. If it's even the right kind. An early birthday present."

"Next Saturday?"

"That'd be fine, James." She set the wrench next to one of the plates Mary had set and looked the table over.

"Oh, really, I couldn't," she said when James suggested she stay for dinner. "I'm on a diet." She lowered her glasses and looked at the table again. "Oh. Salad."

"And hamburgers and hot dogs," said Hannah. "Not a gourmet night tonight, I'm afraid."

"Well, maybe I will stay. You always make such tiny hamburgers. One couldn't hurt."

She sat in her usual spot, next to James. She lifted

a hamburger from the plate using only her thumb and first two fingers. "Pass the ketchup, please, if you will, Jack," Addy said. There were two ketchups on the table, the squeezy one and the bottle. Jack handed Addy the bottle. She poured a thick circular ribbon on top of her hamburger, and when she turned the bottle upright, a glob dripped over the rim. She held it away from her to get a better look, then licked the rim, turning the bottle to make sure she got all the excess ketchup with her tongue before setting the bottle back on the table.

"Do you remember that time we saw Anita O'Day, James?"

"Who's that?" asked Jack.

"Mr. Wooten," Hannah said suddenly, and tipped her glass to Colleen, who clapped her hands once, held her open palms over her plate, and swung with a jazzy "*Cha koom cha boom pow*," and then sang in her fine, dusky voice the first few lines of "Is You Is or Is You Ain't My Baby."

"Oh, I love that one," said Jack.

Hannah handed the squeezy ketchup to James and, now a bit misty-eyed, said to Colleen, "I love it when you sing."

"You're kidding!" said Mary to Addy. "You saw her live?"

"When we were young, we saw all kinds of people.

We used to go over to Baker's Keyboard Lounge on Eight Mile and Livernois every Friday. Also, the Fox Theater, depending on who was playing. We saw Elvis at the Fox the one time." She swiveled her attention from James to each one of his children as she spoke. "This was around 1955, I guess? Which means you were, what, twenty-two, James?"

"Yep."

"And so then I was twenty-five. We were just a few years older than Jack and Mary are now. Goodness."

"Really?" Colleen said.

James nodded.

"But the time I'm talking about is when Anita O'Day was in town. Your father sang with her, and she invited us back to a party at her friend's house. He was some kind of professor at Wayne State, or something."

"No way," Colleen said.

Addy's shoulder dipped down. She leaned to the left as if straining to pick something up off the floor, and let out a *thrapp* of gas. Jack unleashed a cough of laughter; Mary joined in, and said, "I know! Dad, that's amazing! Anita O'Day!" and then they were all free to laugh.

Addy, who had righted herself, laughed, too, and nodded. "Oh yes. Of course, she didn't cotton to me at all, but I think she fancied your father here.

He could have had any woman. He could have had a career. Been a big star."

"Not likely," said James. "I didn't exactly sing with her. She was playful. When she announced she was going to sing 'Stella by Starlight,' she said it sounds better sung by a man. Then she said, 'Does anybody know this song?' We happened to have been at a table near the front that night, and I clapped. Then she said, 'Does anybody who can *sing* know this song?'"

"So I raised my hand and pointed to James," Addy said. "She took one look at him in his suit and tie, his little hat sitting on the table, and she walked right over to him and said, 'Let's give it a shot.'"

"I sang the opening, then sat down and gave the stage back to her."

"I don't know that song," said Colleen.

"Oh, sing it, James. Do," said Addy.

"Come on," said James, shaking his head.

"Really. Don't be impossible," said Addy. "We rarely hear you sing anymore."

James laughed and finally, in his deep mellow voice, sang to Hannah, who, with the second wine bottle three quarters gone, was fully lit and glowing, "*That's Stella by starlight / And not a dream / My heart and I agree / She's everything on this earth to me.*"

"Oh." Addy clutched his arm for a moment. "It was a big success, even though her version was slightly different. And afterwards, that's when she invited us to the party. There were all kinds of people there. It was in the Park Shelton, this big building on Woodward and Kirby. We parked far away for some reason and had to walk five or six blocks. Well, we were younger then, right, James?"

"Her professor friend's apartment was quite a place. Huge apartment, on the eighth floor with a view that looked out over the Detroit Institute of Arts. He told me his rent was seventy-five dollars a month."

"All I remember is all those crazy African blankets everywhere," said Addy.

"I think they were Navajo."

Addy brushed the air with the back of her hand. "Same difference."

"We didn't stay long," James said. "It got too crowded. And so damned hot. Middle of summer, and just a fan in the window."

"And she had a fight with the man," said Addy. "The professor. I was in the bathroom, and I heard arguing. I'm sure it was coming from the bedroom. I couldn't hear what they were saying, but the tone of it was *not* friendly. And then, just as I was coming out of the bathroom, the bedroom door opened and out comes Anita with the man right behind, both their mouths clamped tight. The man goes back out to the party and Anita walks up to this other fellow, says something, and they both leave."

"You don't really know what was going on there, Addy," James said. "That lady had lots of problems."

"But so the interesting part is that after the party we went to Mario's, where we'd parked the car, and who is there but Anita O'Day with the new man."

"Maybe it was just her brother," Hannah said slowly, and quietly.

"I don't think so," said Addy. "We kept looking to see if the professor would come in, or if anybody else from the party was there, but it was just the two of them, very cozy. I wanted to go over and say hello, but James said no."

Addy paused, seemed to think for a moment, then said, "They were over near the private room in the back, but you need at least a party of twelve to go back there." She turned to Jack and said, "That's why we'll be out in front for your father's birthday party next month. We can show you where Anita O'Day sat."

The silence spread itself thin, and then Hannah quietly said, "Oh."

"I know I'm not supposed to say anything, James, but we *are* family. There's no need for secrets, right?"

"Oh," Hannah said again. She sank into the word, and took another sip of wine. James waited for more of a reaction, but Hannah swallowed her disappointment.

The wine and Valium met, wove their warm veil around her, and without moving at all, she withdrew from him completely. If she had been a mean drunk like his father, or an ugly drunk, it might have been easier for James to understand her and her problem. But she was a sweet, maudlin drunk, and somehow he loved her even more because of it. He could have given in, he could have told Addy right then and there that his place was with the family he had made, rather than the one he was simply born into, and that he wanted to spend his birthday right here at home, at the dinner table with his real family. But where a birthday party is held is such a small, silly thing, and Addy, so used to controlling everything and everyone except herself, sat big, indomitable, and triumphant in her chair, and James said nothing. *This will pass,* he thought. *Tomorrow is Monday, and Hannah will either be angry or not. We'll talk it through when we get home from work.*

In the future, the memory of Hannah's defeated expression would cut him much the way her expression when she'd asserted her desperate love for him had cut him. Only after Hannah was gone would James become aware of the two kinds of memory: the kind over which he had control and which he could summon on reflection; and the other unruly, many-tentacled thing that crystallized suddenly in unsuspecting moments of his present life. Around the central memory of Hannah would spike this look of defeat, that look of desperation, the feel of her hip bone, her laugh, the sound of her scratchy, unmoored voice when she sang, the smell of her hair freshly washed with her favorite wheat germ oil and honey shampoo. The memories would float up and turn to show their many facets all through his life. They would prick him at her funeral; they would cut him again four years later at Jack's funeral with all Jack's pretty boy friends circling around them, thin and blank-faced as ghosts; and again when Mary moved away to New York; he'd feel a shaft of it while watching Colleen slowly grow enormous like Addy; and another jab when, ten years down the road, he'd find Addy face down in her kitchen, dead of a heart attack, and stewing in a week of decay. He didn't know yet that he'd spend the next year pushing his children away, searching for his wife among the scrawls she'd left in the pages of the many books she'd read, or that there would come a moment when he'd lift his head from those books to find that his wife had been an ordinary woman; she'd left no message for him, she would not speak to him from the grave. At the end of that first year, he'd return to his family, shy, a little ashamed, and exhausted, but he'd find that while he was gone, they'd changed too. His children had become adults with their own joys and fears and accomplishments and miseries, and they had learned no longer to need him as much. Especially Jack. James would never understand it. Mary and Colleen tried to help him feel less of a failure as a father, to no avail. It would be the keen afterglow of Hannah's haunting love that guided him through the agonizing ugliness of watching their lovely boy's once strong body rot alive, and wither to nothing.

But of course, on this night he was just living his life, as we all do, not knowing or caring if the present moment would slip away into the blur that makes up most of our lives, or lodge in the latticework of memory to become another clear, sharp pang that periodically resurfaces in some unrelated, unsuspected future.

He let the moment pass. Addy, pinky finger upraised, took another hamburger to her plate. Jack, Colleen, and Mary complimented their mother on the dinner. Hannah combed her fingers through the hair above her left ear, uncovering the silver spot for a moment. She swirled her wine, her face flushed, her eyes unfocused and glistening.

Addy left shortly after dinner. Colleen cleared the table while Jack and Mary did the dishes, and Hannah slipped off to bed.

That night, James lay down next to Hannah, his nose buried in her hair, and lay his hand over the smooth skin at her hip. They nuzzled into the familiar hollows of each other's bodies. The next day, James would wake before her, and by the time he was out of the shower, she'd be up. He'd kiss her forehead to avoid her morning breath. They'd both go to work and do all the forgettable things we all do to fill our days.

But for now, on that Sunday night, he wanted to explain that it was because Hannah was everything to him that he gave Addy her small victories. As usual, what he felt was too big and too complicated to put into words, so he said nothing. Since she was already asleep, he thought it best to let it go. He told himself all the things he always told himself. *She'll figure it out sooner or later on her own. It's foolish to worry about such a small thing. Everything will work itself out.* He decided not to think too much about it, and then, in those last few moments before drifting off to sleep, James stopped thinking completely. He let his senses take over to register the dumb animal comforts that lull us into the night. He dissolved into the smell of his wife's hair, the feel of her heat warming him under the covers. It was March, and still freezing. The rafters creaked, the furnace squawked, his children rumbled and thrummed on the floor below, and James let go, slipping off to sleep in relative peace amid the sounds of the house settling around him.

Starlight

"No moon tonight."

"Of course there's a moon, Hannah, we just can't see it," says Marianne even while my head's still tilted at the milky sky, looking. "Or it's out of phase."

Thank you, Mrs. Galileo, I want to say, but I just smile and squeeze her arm and let her think she's as smart as she thinks she is. The sky is layers of gray and black clouds that slide back and forth over one another, change shapes, and move along. No. No moon tonight.

"G'night, all. See you tomorrow."

I shouldn't have said to the girls that I wanted to kill James. I'll make it up to him when I get home. I can't keep anything against him when I feel so lovely like this.

Colder than this morning. Where are my keys? Funny how when the fresh air hits you, the alcohol does too. I always think it'll be the other way around, that the cold air will clear your head, but instead it fluffs that deep good feeling so it swells and shoots up into my head to settle all pretty like a fresh layer of snow. Very nice.

What am I looking for? Keys. Shite. Ha. Landed right on the ice. Is it that cold? But at least they didn't slip under the car. Wouldn't that be a pretty picture, me on my knees with my ass in the air looking for keys under my car in the parking lot of the local "establishment." The kids would have a conniption. Mary and Jack would laugh, but I'd get nothing but the fish-eye from Colleen. Or maybe not. She's my daughter after all and she's not always as bad as Addy, but then who is.

"Oh, Marianne! No, I'm okay, just dropped my keys. Sure, I'm fine. No, no, I'm fine, really. Have a good night. Yes, it's freezing. Ha! Yes, antifreeze. Ha! Very clever. Got them now, see? Take care. Drive carefully. Yes, yes. Bye now."

Oof. There.

Oh, it is cold. Seat's like ice. Sit here and warm up a bit, keep the windows from fogging. Jesus, I hope Addy's not there again when I get home. Feel like a visitor in my own home. Still can't believe she's his real sister. If it weren't for that gigantic nose, I'd think she was adopted. Looks so much better on him, as does everything. Not a pat of fat anywhere on James and her big as a load of hay. He got the looks and the sweet disposition, so quiet and gentle and intense, and her just a big block of nothing much. Which I suppose is reason enough to be kind to her, poor thing. Unhappy. Although she tells James it's me who's unhappy. *If ever I'm unhappy, you'll be the first to know*, I told James. *You, the kids. Any woman would be crazy to be unhappy with you. I drink because I like the TASTE, and that's it.* That woman could make a cyclone out of a hiccup. If a woman can't have a drink now and again well life would just be one long dull drag toward the grave. I've my own wages so it's not that I'm taking food out of the kids' mouths or clothes off their backs for Christ's sake. It's only Addy has the problem with it. Has a problem with me more like, eyeballing everything in the house like I'm robbing James blind. *Such expensive toilet paper*, she says, as if we should still be crumpling newspaper for it like they did on the farm. Well, if ever it became a problem, of course I'd stop, but it's only out with the girls at school once or twice a week and then only my wine with dinner at home. She's not civilized. The French and Italians drink wine morning, noon, and night, and Criminy, it's not a meal without wine, although James doesn't partake as much. He's so wiry and delicate almost, which is just another thing to love about him. I know he worries about me. He doesn't say much, but I can see it. Well, he loves me, it's natural, isn't it. Of course it is. And he's so good to me.

He's no John DeLorean to be sure, but Sally says

electricians make more than some doctors, and does James know anyone young and good-looking and available she could meet. Fat chance for fat Sally, poor thing. *A good man is a good man*, Sally says, *but a good man who can supplement the household cupboards is better, and that's what I need because, hmmpph, to pay eighth grade teachers almost the same as what secretaries make, well*, she says, which was a dig at me until she realized she was talking right to my face. I could have said, *You'd need a millionaire to keep your cupboards full by the looks of your backside*, but of course I didn't. And why shouldn't I make almost as much as she does? I keep that school running. Sister Theodore couldn't keep St. Benedict's all in order by herself, and what about the nuns? Beggars scrape together more coins than those nuns do, although it's true the sisters have free room and board for life, but they have to live in that house all together, only women, and that'd be penance enough for me to be sure. Besides the chastity thing. I wonder if it's a burden or a relief for most of them. Some women say they don't like it at all. *All that mess and bother, for what?* says Marianne. But I think it's just her way of putting on some Polly Purebread act to make like she's better than other people. She's always going on about *propriety* or some damn thing, but how can not having fun in bed with your own husband make you a better person? Just the opposite, as far as I'm concerned.

Oh, the days James and I had! The days, the days. The kids are lovely to be sure, but wasn't it grand before. S'pose I could have done more with them, but they are coming up okay, and kids're a bit like weeds anyway, thank God: hard to kill and they come up mostly on their own without much tending.

That's nice, the heat. I could fall asleep right here practically. Crystals on the windshield almost all melted. Pretty. Almost sad to see them go. Wipers on and WHOOSH! Bye-bye to the stars in my eyes.

What's the name again of that drink? Starscraper? No. Stardust. Don't know. Oh, isn't that silly and here we've been having it nearly every week the past month. Black Sambuca and vodka. Never seen anything like it. I can still taste the licorice. That is really something. Something special. And that little curl of lemon on the rim. That's the starlight, that handsome young waiter said. That's it: Starlight Martini. Lemon strip of starlight atop the rim and the purple black swirl underneath like the night. Very clever. And what's a good drink but just a bit of light on an otherwise drear day? Sure no one can deny me that, like that Starlight thingy. They call it that for a reason, right? Better than the rotgut hooch they used to have to drink in the old days. Funny, the names they come up with: white lightning, moonshine. Brilliant. Starlight and moonshine, that's what the world needs more of, I say. Light in darkness.

I do wish the kids were old enough to drink, we'd have a grand time. Well, I suppose Mary and Colleen are. Jack's still only in high school, but maybe he does already. I don't think so, he'd tell me. He's like James, quiet and concentrated and deliberate, but still funny. Mary's quite the good-time girl too, but Jack's funnier than all of us. That time I told them about one of the teachers who had the baby born with his intestines outside rather than in and how they had to do major surgery on the poor little thing to get everything back in place. When I said they'd have to keep him in the hospital for a long time, James asked, *How long?* and Jack said, *Well, I guess until he gets his shit together*, and we all laughed so hard. So witty, but he's also the most serious, too. Intense. It takes him a while, but sooner or later he zeroes in and goes right to the nub of it. He's the most truthful of all my kids. A little too truthful sometimes. Like when he was little, stroking Addy's cheek and being a little doll, then out he comes with, *Ma's right, fat people like you really do have lovely skin.* He thought he was giving her a compliment. Jesus, I could have throttled him. She laughed but I know she was hurt. I felt horrible. He is a dear. Whenever there's a row in the house, Jack has the knack of stepping into the middle to defuse it, especially between the girls.

Mary'd just as soon walk away and be done with it, but Colleen just keeps at it. She's so sensitive, although she puts on a hard front and gets vicious. Which is odd. When she's not mad, she's straitlaced and buttoned up, except when she sings. Everyone says she looks like me, but it's only our hair and boobs they're talking about. She's so full and lovely, still young and slim, but she'll need to watch it, I'm afraid. Addy was once young and slim too, though you'd never know it to look at her now. I'd hate to think that side of his family got into any of our kids, but Colleen can get nasty when she wants, and she reminds me too much of Addy, although I'd never say so to her. Never looks at her own faults to try to get past them as Mary and Jack do. Everything always someone else's fault, not hers, and likes to stir the pot to get an argument going.

What time is it? Just past five o'clock and coming on dark already, or maybe that's from the storm clouds blowing in and out. I suppose we did start a tad early, but it's not that often we get half the day off. Report card day. All the little ones so nervous and happy at the same time, it makes me laugh. Still, they're glad for any reason to get a half day at school, especially on a Monday. Sister Theodore wanted to make report card day on the twenty-sixth, which is her name day, so she could get a little time off for herself. She needed the get-go from Father Walsh, but they get along like two cats tied up in a gunnysack. He never misses a chance to remind her that Saint Theodore had his tongue cut off as a martyr and that she should take his full example. *Yes*, she says, *but it was because he was on God's side that he lost his tongue*. And then Father, *Even so*, with that smirk of his, and that really scorches her. Still, she's the principal, she should be able to make decisions about the school herself. Did she take her name day last year? It should be the same day every year. Or rather a different day every year except for leap year. So it would skip a day or repeat a day on leap year, I wonder which it is.

Jack'll be home by now. Breaks my heart sometimes, I love him so much. It's not right to love one more than the others, but all mothers do really, no matter what they say. Can't help it, they're just people. Sometimes I watch him when he doesn't know I'm looking and I just about bust. He'll be washing dishes or sweeping the floor or taking off his loafers to put on the slippers he keeps by the front door so he won't track dirt through the house. And then he'll look up, like he knows what I'm thinking, and he'll smile that big smile of his, or shuffle over in his slippers *shush, shush, shush* to kiss me. It's because he's the boy, I imagine. Only natural. I worry about him, though. He can be hard as nails and then cry at a soap commercial. He told me once, *I should be a better person*, but I had no idea what he was talking or where he got such a dumb notion that he wasn't.

You smother that boy, Addy says. *That's no way to make a man.* As if there's something wrong with loving my son. She doesn't see she does the same thing with James, in her own coarse way.

Okay, stop. The more riled up I get about Addy, the more she wins. If she's in my thoughts, then she's captured me. It's like I'm her slave, she's got me carrying her around with me all the live-long day, replaying everything she does and says, and I won't let her and her nasty ways win. Get your mind otherwise occupied, Hannah. It does no good to fester over her and I will NOT.

Not, I'll not, carrion comfort, despair, not feast on thee. Not untwist—slack they may be—these last strands of man in me.

No, I don't like that one. Too morbid.

Glory be to God for dappled things. For skies of couple-color as a brinded cow.

Brinded. What does that word mean? I always mean to look it up, a thousand times, and a thousand and one times I forget again. Maybe he meant branded or something.

Too warm now. Turn that down. Okay, let's go. No one behind me. Oop. Must be the curb. Lot almost empty back here. The Back Stage, wonder why they call it that. Oh. Telephone pole. How did that get there? No harm. Anyway, that's why they're called bumpers. I should go to that store to get that pen for James's birthday while I remember. Southfield and Something Mile Road. I guess take Six Mile to Southfield. Not as busy as Eight Mile, then turn and just keep my eyes peeled. Wait for the traffic to go by a little more before slipping in. Oh cripe, I'll have to get all the way over to do that turn around thing. Hate that.

Here we go.

Why we have to come all the way back here to Woodward and Six Mile for a drink, I don't know. It's a terrible neighborhood. If I broke down, I might be in real trouble over here. It's for Sally, of course. Because she lives in Ferndale, it's just a straight shot down Woodward for her. She heard about the place from her friend, Arthur, the one with all the poodles. *Most of the waiters there are funny boys*, Marianne says, *and a lot of the patrons too, just don't tell the Sisters.* I didn't understand and said, *It's not a sin, nuns are allowed to drink and laugh too*, but Marianne laughed and said, *That's not really the point, Hannah*, and then after we got there the first time, I sort of saw what she meant, but most of the young men there were well-dressed and mannerly. *They look as normal as Jack or any of his friends to me*, I said, and Marianne smiled that shit-eating smile of hers and I wanted to spit in her face, but I just said, *It's hard to tell anybody's problems just by looking at them*, and I returned her shit-eating grin and let it go at that. She'll make up anything just to cause a little drama. Well, they do call this place Back Stage, so I guess she thinks it's okay to try be dramatic here. It is nice, though, isn't it. All done up with those pretty green walls with the green-black trim and old-fashioned lanterns for lights. Sophisticated and warm, I don't know any other place in Detroit like it. Makes you feel like you're in a whole 'nother world altogether. Mostly men, but feel safe. Then step out and drive down Six Mile like this and it's all run-down houses, liquor stores, pawn shops, sex shops, closed businesses, and churches, and people—men and women both—stumbling around with no light in their eyes. Scary. Get back to Southfield and turn right to get to that pen store or whatever it is. Too expensive for a silly pen, but why shouldn't he have something nice, even if it's just for crossword puzzles.

At least Six Mile's not all rush and bustle like Eight Mile.

I should find out how to make that Starlight drink. Just to look at it, it's everything I want: a big black swirl of the dark quiet with a little fleck of light far away at the top. I couldn't do it every night on top of the wine. Maybe I'll have people over at Easter and instead of black jellybeans I'll introduce the Starlight

Martini as my new drink. If ever there was a drink that said Hannah Grace Fallon I don't know what else it would be. It's amazing no one ever thought of it until now. Well, I suppose they did, it's just that I'd never heard of it. Think of all the things out there yet to discover and me sitting here dumb as a doorknob not knowing any of it.

I may not be as smart as a teacher, but Marianne shouldn't act like that. She gets sort of nasty when she's not drinking. She's another who likes to start things. Everyone's waiting to see what will happen to poor crazy Sister Philomena, after she stripped that boy naked in front of her fourth grade class to spank him, but none of us much talk about it. She's been off her rocker for a while, but I feel sorry for her. Sister Theodore says they find tuna sandwiches, boiled eggs, even cottage cheese hidden under Philomena's bed from months ago. They knew the stink was from her, but they didn't know why. Thought it might be something feminine until Sister Theodore had the whole house scrubbed and they found months' worth of spoiled food under the bed and even under the mattress. *What do you think'll happen to Philomena?* Marianne asks me right in front of all the other lay teachers, when she knows I can't divulge diocese information. *If I could scry things like that, I'd be a rich woman,* I said. *Scry*, Marianne says. *How do you know a word like that?* As if I'd spent my life under a pile of rotten logs. I said it because it's a funny-sounding word and I've always liked it. *It's just a word, Marianne. I imagine I learned it somewhere around fifth grade. If you think it's so special, maybe you can put it in your Vocab Words for the Week*, as she likes to call it. *I will*, she said, *thanks*, and it surprised us both. I think she really was grateful and maybe showed her I'm not such a big dummy as she thought, even if I am just a secretary and don't have a degree like she does.

Southfield? Fine. Turn and watch. It's got to be near Nine or Ten Mile, no more than Eleven to be sure.

The lights! My, they whiz past. Whiz! If they were stars instead of cars it'd all be so peaceful. It'll be nice to sleep tonight; I'll think of lights bright, twinkling, whizzing, so beautiful it almost hurts. I have no worries when the stars shine like that, especially in winter. The stars are big and bright but there's more black space than there are stars. In between it must be so dark and cold and very still. All peace and no razzle. That's how it felt when James and I first met, all the razzle-fizz in my nerves settled and I felt we could live in our own heavenly cool stillness with no one to bother us and that was true love. But then of course work and chores, and before we knew it the kids, which is what I knew I was supposed to do, and the next time I could draw my breath the deep calm of true love disappeared and it was all razzle and chores and Addy butting in and no one would leave me alone, and it was hard to even read a book. That time I broke down when Jack was still just a baby, James was so good. He bought me books and at night in bed when we were too tired for the other thing, or usually after it when we were flushed with the high of it, he'd read to me, and then I'd take over and read him to sleep and oh it was glorious. He got me that special light I could keep on so he could sleep while I read, and it was good. But then because of the money and such, I got the job at St. Benedict's and the ones who weren't nuns were so nice and we'd go for drinks just like tonight and it used to be just wine, that was always grand, and then Marianne bought us the round of Starlight Martinis, and one sip of that and that was love all over again. Lovely.

Oops. Sorry! Big deal, a little out of my lane. We're stopped at a light anyway, you're not going anywhere. Relax, buddy.

I am dog tired. Maybe shouldn't have had that third one, but it tastes so good and you forget about the booze in it, don't you. Good Gow, everybody always beeping all the time. Oh. Green. Okay okay okay. Criminy, is that rain or snow? Ah, yes, snow. Starts and stops. It's already March almost April. I guess by May we'll be safe. These lights so pretty lighting up the snow.

Oof. This Starlight thing'll be better than Valium for sleep, although I only use it for nerves now instead of sleep. They took it away from me then, that was a horrible time, and all because I needed some rest. I took that big lot of Valium, but all I did was sleep and sleep and that's all I really wanted I guess, just to sleep, but the doctor said if James hadn't brought me in to get my stomach pumped that could've been it. What if I did? There'd be sadness, I hope, but it would pass, it always does. When Dad died, I thought I'd die too, but I didn't. I had James and the kids, which helped I suppose, but then I lost it after Ma went. I hope there's something after, there has to be, who could bear it otherwise if this was it? They say it's the worst sin because it's the loss of hope, but any god worth his salt would know we're all imperfect humans by definition so of course he'd have to forgive it. It's a million times better than killing somebody else, or even robbery.

Addy says it's a sin to feel that way. Perhaps it is, but how can it be a sin to *feel* something? It's not like I can help it. *You could help it*, Addy said, *if you tried*. She thinks I'm selfish and I suppose if I were honest, I am, but what's a body to do? Anyway, we're all sinners, and she should talk. *It's a sin to be angry and mean all the time too*, I said, *but that never stopped you*. That shut her up for a while, but James said I should never have said it and he was right, but I wasn't myself then and I told him to tell her so, and he said he already did.

"Despair" is such a funny word. Despair. Despair. Despair of pants makes you look fat! What is it the Jews had? Despair. Despair. Diaspora! Scattered throughout the earth. Like Adam and Eve after the apple. But what did the Jews do that they had to scatter? Still, despair. Sure everyone feels it sometimes, I mean how can you not? If you're lucky like I am, you meet someone and marry, then kids, they grow up, you grow old and die and what's the point of it all anyway? How can a body not despair if you think about it? It's the most natural thing in the world, but nobody wants to admit it. What difference if I died fifteen years ago or fifteen years from now? It's all the same, isn't it? Then there's the whole heaven thing, but that's just a bunch of foolishness really. I guess that's why it's a sin, because if you think too hard about it all then you doubt God, which is a pretty big sin, after all. But how can there be Jews and Muslims and Christians and Hindus and Greeks and Romans and Egyptians and the Irish too, way back, Druids, that's it. They all believed theirs was the one true way and they killed people who didn't believe them, but how can only one be right all through time? It's a little crazy if you ask me, but they are good stories. Addy wouldn't understand.

She's so quick to get up on her high horse about religion like she did that one night last summer talking about God and faith and right and wrong. She's one of those who thinks talking about God makes you smart or good or interesting when she's none of the three to begin with. Going to church is one thing but going on and on about Jesus and miracles and the wrath of God is a little much, but she was all up in arms about a priest and a nun in her parish who left to get married. *It's a desecration of the sacred trust*, she said. *Nuns nowadays going around wearing normal clothes instead of traditional habits. You don't even know who's who or what's what, so of course they'll tempt a priest right out of their vocation. That young Sister Pauline and Father Tim have an affair, announce it in church, and run off together—both of them shameless. The whole time lying through their teeth—or their zippers or whatever. Disgusting. Making us think they're all fine and holy when all the while . . .*

They're just people like the rest of us, I said.

Like who? she says, and sits back in her chair giving me the stink-eye. *I know I don't go around pretending I'm something I'm not. I don't want priests and nuns to be like us. They should be better. Examples. Hmmpph. Some example, rumpling the sheets in the house of God and smiling at us in the morning like the cat that ate the canary. Weak willed*, she said, looking straight at me.

And then Jack popped in with that thing about the Druids because he was doing a report on them for school. *Do you know they think the word for "druid" was the same in ancient Irish as the word for "nun," and also maybe for the words "oak" and "wren"?* he said in his sweet, quiet way. *Both women and men could become Druids, but they had to study for it for twenty years. Trouble is, we don't really know that much about them except from reports by Julius Caesar because they had an oral tradition rather than written.* It didn't have anything to do with anything Addy was saying, but his sweet wonder at it charmed us all into listening to him rather than bickering with each other. I was sure Addy would circle back to her own grievance like she always does, but she never did and I credit Jack for making her forget.

I suppose I should be ashamed of myself for raising the kids Catholic and working at the school when I have doubts, but it's good to have a basis of some sort: Be nice to people, don't kill, don't lie. Well, I haven't done too well on that last one, but all the truth all the time wouldn't just be impossible, but unbearable too. Even President Carter admitted he lusted in his heart for other women and it caused a big scandal, but no one seems to be grateful that he was honest about it. If I had the courage to tell every truth in my heart at every moment, it would hurt too many people. Which means I am a liar and a fake. Big news. But what's the point of living if it's all lies? Does anyone really wonder why a person might despair?

That's the pen place there. How about that? That's what it's called: The Pen Place. Ha! Just pop in. I hate these strip malls, there's never a good place to park with enough room. Go around back of it and look. It gets harder every year to get a good gift. You want something that means something, and if it's really useful that helps, although if it's pretty enough, useful doesn't matter quite so much. Sally says buy myself a sexy slip for his birthday, but that's a single woman's idea of sexy. There's a spot. Well, I suppose two could fit here, but I'll just be a minute.

Stopped snowing. Clouds clearing, but that freezing wind would cut you in two.

Why do they have to have the lights so blaring in all these places, it's not like we're all blind. Back counter.

"Hello."

"Hi, yes. A pen. For my husband."

"All righty. Do you have a particular kind of pen in mind?"

"Green. It was green. It was at this counter we saw it. With a skinny tip."

"Skinny tip?"

"So he can do the crossword."

"Fine point, you mean? Fountain or ball point?"

"That's it. Bull pen. Fine pull. Yes. The green. Lotta money for a faint smidge of steel and ink. Still, it's pretty, isn't it?"

"Very, ma'am. If you could just . . ."

"Need to find my . . ."

"Ma'am?"

"Where's the cashier?"

"I'm ringing you up here. That's eighty-two fifty."

". . ."

"Ma'am?"

"What? Yes. Don't have my reading glasses. Lights so bright in here, you can hardly see. Makes a person dizzy just to stand here. Is that it?"

"This is a Sears charge. We take MasterCard, Visa, and cash."

"Who carries around that kind of cash?"

"Some people do, ma'am."

"Don't be silly. Of course. My wallet. Here. It's in there somewhere."

"This one, ma'am."

"Yes, yes. Go on. Take it."

"Here we go. Here's your card. I'll put it back in your wallet. Right in the front."

"Fine, fine. Thank you. Good night."

"Ma'am? You need to sign, please."

"Oh, pigs in heaven, yes. Fine. Here we go, and that's that. Wallet, purse. 'Night. Thank you."

"Ma'am."

Silly little snot-nosed chits, ma'amming me to death. They should teach them in cashier school not to make customers feel like they're idiots. Oo, that's a bitter wind. The sky's cleared up in bits. Oh, the moon! Half-moon. Never know whether it's coming or going. Keys, keys, keys. Shite and Shinola, I need a smaller bag, where do they get to?

"Ma'am? Excuse me, ma'am? You left these on the counter."

"Oh, sweet sassafras! I was just looking for those. Oh, good God, and the pen too. Thank you. Isn't the moon lovely, though, through those feathery clouds?"

"Sorry, ma'am, but you're okay, right? Or we could call someone if you needed . . ."

"Yes. I mean, no. I mean I'm fine, of course I'm fine. I just forgot my keys is all. Much thanks. Have a good night and thanks again."

"You too, ma'am. You have a good night too. And you're right. The moon is beautiful. I always forget to look for it. Good night."

How about that. She's not such a bad girl after all. Just doing her job. Sort of sweet. Too bad about the pimply complexion, though. Probably has a hard time with people because of it. Sort of off-putting having to stare at that red splotchy mug and try to pretend not to notice.

Oof. Car still warm at least. Back on the trail. Southfield, this is? Too many big roads. So much traffic. Go straight back down Southfield, then get back to the school and take Outer Drive for the scenic route home. Can I do that from here? Try anyway. Hate that big overpass to I-96, everything rush rush zoom zoom.

Isn't it funny about driving? It can be one of the best parts of my day so long as no other cars are around. If I drive someplace new, it's harder to think because you have to figure out what to do and pay attention where to go. The best drives are in your own familiar area with no traffic, just you and the car and the road and your thoughts. Racing through the wind, flying in a big machine that makes you feel like you're sitting like a queen but really you're flying through space at fifty miles an hour or more. Driving, I can be all by myself. Quiet. Some people need to talk all the time and can never shut up, as if silence is a special danger to them. Afraid they'll discover something they never really wanted to know. There are times behind the wheel when I think I could just keep driving. Land somewhere from out of the blue, get an apartment, a job cleaning a motel or something, where I don't have to see anybody or talk to anybody and I can just rest.

If I could do that and never come back, or come back whenever I wanted and then go away again when I needed to, and if everybody understood, that would be grand. But it doesn't work that way.

Anyway, I do love them, and I'd probably regret it. God knows I've had my moods where I thought I wanted something, went for it, and regretted it severely afterward. That whole Sammy Issa affair. James never found out. I'd die if he ever did, not just because I love him so much, but because I didn't know how much I loved him until after. That was just after Jack was born and I felt all lumpy and tender and ugly not because of anything James said or did, but because of me. And then, *zoom*, there was Sammy in his mechanics overalls and those sleepy Lebanese eyes and that low deep gentle voice complimenting me every time I came in for gas or an oil change or a bag of rock salt or a coffee. We did it only just the two times, just after James started at Greenfield Village and had to work all that overtime because he was new. And I told Addy I had to go out or I'd lose my mind and she watched the kids. I've never seen a man with such smooth skin, chest hairless as polished stone, and before that I'd thought all Arab men were hairy. *Habibi*, he called me. And it felt so good, so different from James, not better, but different. Exciting. And then the last time he held me and told me he loved me and I said immediately, *Oh no, I love James,* just like that without thinking. And I think that and the crying jag scared the life out of him, which is just as well because we both saw it was no good. I was glad it was over but glad I did it too so that I found out what I needed to find out, but I was so tired and so riled up at the same time, and that's when I took the Valium and it didn't seem to work so I took more and a little more just to sleep. After all that, it took me a while before I could do it again with James, but I think he thought it was all an extended postpartum thing, what with all the tears and sleeping and my moods, but he was patient and after I got my next period, I felt more pure, and then it was better than ever with James and that's when he got that night light for me to read by.

I do love James, but I also love to be left alone sometimes, and I don't think he'll ever fully understand that.

I asked him the one time if we could move somewhere quiet and peaceful but he got that hurt look on his face and said, *Are you not happy?* I couldn't answer, not because I was or wasn't happy but because I didn't think of it like that. *I've got a good job here,* he said, *at Greenfield Village, the union, a pension. I don't know where I'd find the same, especially now with the auto plants laying people off and those people looking for jobs now.* I knew he was right, but then he said, *And then there's Addy*, and I could have spit, and he saw it in my face. *She's my sister*, he said, *and she's all alone.* I said, *She's all alone by her own choice*, but I know what he means. You can't be all alone all the time, we need other people. And anyway, other people show us who we really are. Naturally we stick closest to the people who bring out the best in us, those who can take what we have to give. James is a great gift-getter. For our twenty-fifth anniversary I got him that little candle holder made of rock salt to remind him of our first date at the salt mine. He actually cried. I thought for a minute that he was disappointed, but then I knew it was exactly the right thing. We spent the night in the hotel at the Renaissance Center way up in a room on the seventy-second floor overlooking the river. We turned out the lights and lit the candle in it, and it glowed so nice and pink with the candle inside and we did it with the shades open, just the sky and the rock salt candle as our only light. He'll like the pen.

Here's school. Back on track so soon. Outer Drive is like riding a snake home. This damn street has so many twists and turns, it's a wonder I don't end up in Ohio. All the Mile Roads are in order, but Outer Drive twists through them all and I never really get how. Did I pass Six Mile yet? What's that sign say? Oh Christ, it's coming down again, fluffy and white now. Jesus, Mary, and Joseph, why do they make signs like that so it's all blurry in the night? I get all mixed up. Maybe that's it coming up. By the looks of the houses, no, not yet. Well, maybe. Strange that. How the houses change so. So grand and majestic, oh yes, here we are, and this is Rosedale Park. Amazing. It's like mansions they are here. Up by school it's nothing much, then Rosedale houses so big and fancy like movie stars, then down by us the houses so small and plain and poor looking. I suppose compared to those in Rosedale Park, we are poor. But we do okay, we have clothes and food and cars to get around. You'd think there'd be a mark, a clear point where the houses go from rich to poor, but I always miss it.

I drive this road five days a week for years on end and sometimes it all seems brand new. Hard to pay sufficient attention to every detail all the time. I suppose you'd explode if you did, there's so much wonder in the world. Addy says that's why she does the miniatures, so she can slow down and pay more attention to the world, but if that were true she'd see how ridiculous she makes herself with her bully ways. If she moved any slower, you'd mistake her for Stonehenge. She does really notice things. She's constantly explaining about the buildings we see in Detroit, cornices and arches and columns and balustrades and porticoes and such, which is interesting for a while, but she does go on. I can only listen to that kind of stuff for a little while before I get bored, which is my shortcoming, I know. And she's so very detailed making her little dioramas or whatever they're called. She made us that beautiful tiny cathedral that we put up on the shelf behind the bar downstairs. Oh Christ, and I moved it for the Christmas party we had when James invited all his work friends, and we didn't invite Addy, so I moved the cathedral she made to make room for more bottles in the bar. I put it on the floor next to the small refrigerator and Jack accidentally set the crate of oranges on top of it and crushed it to bits. He felt so bad, he cried, even though it was really my fault. That was the party where I fell in front of all his friends, and everyone rushed over as if I died or something, *but I'm just a little woozy*, I said, and they all laughed, but it was so embarrassing, maybe more for James than for me. Next time Addy came over and she was in the basement she said, *I don't see the cathedral, I wonder where it went*, but I didn't want to even mention the party, so I lied and said, *I moved it to dust it*, and left it at that, but she said it with that smarmy smile so of course James probably already told her.

I almost envy her. I don't have any kind of talent. Music, people say, but that comes as easy as breathing, it doesn't feel like talent. It's just playing around. And Addy's right, it's not like I could do anything with it, especially with my voice. I'm glad she's got something she likes to keep her busy, and she's good at it. She got an Honorable Mention in that competition last year. Sorry we couldn't go, but that was Siobhan's son's funeral. She's my only cousin and our kids got along so well together when they were little, we had to go. Brian was her oldest boy, two years older than Mary. He was a dancer at the Gaelic League and taught Jack how to do a proper jig, and Jack wanted so much for us to join the Gaelic League, but we really couldn't afford it at the time. Whenever they'd come over, I'd play, and the kids would dance and sing, and it was such a happy time, and then he jumps off a building. What a way to do it, but I guess there is no way that isn't gruesome. Horrible, that. In medical school, and he got arrested at that rest stop off the expressway along with sixteen other men for lewd conduct. Names and pictures in the newspaper and everything under the headline "Gay Sex Sting," and the next day he jumped off the roof of the medical school library. What on earth could he have been thinking? There's a case where he could have lied and we'd have all believed him, at least a little bit, because who would want to believe otherwise? Seems like a hard life. Jack will find a nice girl someday, but she'll have to be special just like James found me.

Don't really understand. They say it goes on all the time, but you never think it'd be anyone you know.

Why in a bathroom, of all places? It's so dirty. Siobhan asked Brian, *Did you do it*, and he said, *Yes.* And him so bright and promising with his future all ahead of him. Father Walsh says, *Kill yourself and you go straight to Hell.* Another reason not to believe all that nonsense. Living is its own hell for some people.

I love how Outer Drive has the boulevard in the middle with the trees and the lawn. Adds a little class. Almost makes you feel like you're in the country.

The nerve of Addy bullying James into agreeing to having his birthday party at Mario's even though I said I wanted to have it at home with nobody but us. I forgive him, but she's a different story. *I know what's best for James*, she's always saying. She thinks it should be her and him and nobody else. It's just weird, but I suppose when I came along, it was hard for her to think of her brother involved in the whole sex thing. I wonder why. Sex is natural and fun, but then part of the fun might be the feeling of naughtiness that goes along with it and makes us want to hide it. Animals don't care, why should we, they do it right out on the front lawn for all the world to see bing bang boom, so why should we be so shy about it? Maybe because it takes us so much longer to do it. But of course there's the fact that we are all just animals that's embarrassing. And you want privacy. Add to that sin and shame and all that, and I can understand why it disturbs people.

Nobody wants to be seen naked or to have people who have no business with them thinking about their naked bits. And even though I've seen the kids naked changing their diapers, nobody wants to imagine other people doing things with their kids, but then when they're adults, they're just like us, so live and let live, I suppose. And the fact that all our fun bits are down there with all our bathroom bits does make it seem dirty.

Poor Siobhan.

But then there's love. It doesn't always work out that way, but when it does, it's better with love. It does bring two people closer together, sharing that secret pleasure, which is exactly why a wife should have more sway over a man than his sister does.

Addy thinks she has some magical key that unlocks James's natural tendency to go quiet and sullen every so often. I don't mind that in him, in fact sometimes I welcome it. We need time to ourselves, but he is fearsome in his sulks. *When are you going to learn not to let the wet clothes sit in the washing machine overnight? Everything smells like mold*, he said the one time. I came back with, *When are you going to learn you can take the clothes out of a washer as well as I can? If you wanted a servant rather than a wife, you should have married that little snivel Ellen Burke back when you had the chance.* He went quiet for the whole weekend that time. Everyone, me, the kids, and even Addy stayed away. He came around gradually, as he always does. That Sunday I laid out a plate of saltines with kippered herring arranged on top the way he likes it for lunch instead of letting him do it himself like usual. I didn't say a thing, just set it on the table and went about my business. If it's a weeknight, I'll set out the bath salts he likes—the one called white musk—and a nail brush for his toes conspicuous on the bathroom counter so he can see it first thing when he goes to pee when he gets home. Then, if I hear him running the bath, I'll wink to the kids to let them know dinner will be a little later, and when he comes to the table, we know he'll be refreshed and the sulk will have lifted.

Addy thinks she's the only one who knows how to handle him, but what do I know, maybe she's right. Or maybe her way is just as good. Hers works for her, mine works for me. Well, for all we know, nothing either of us does has any effect. James is his own man. He's certainly strong enough to handle himself.

I do remember that one time he went off for an entire week in a sulk that no herring or white musk could touch. He asked if he died, would I remarry, and I said, *Of course*. He said it felt like a slap. *That makes me feel about as important as a refrigerator*, he said. *If one breaks down, toss it out and get another. It's easier for women than for men, I guess.* But the point he didn't get was that I love being married, and it's because of him. If he died, I'd be devastated for a while, sure, who wouldn't? But it's because I love him so much and he makes married life so much fun that I'd want to do it again. That's the point: His good example's what spurred me. I wasn't able to get that idea out to him. I hate how it takes me so long to find the words I need to make myself understood. I should tell him that when I get home. No. Bringing up something like that from so long ago might light the fuse again and who knows if I wouldn't lose my words again. Anyway, it's a silly argument. Why worry about something that's never happened. Perhaps I'll tell him if it ever comes up again. I won't bring it up myself. Be stupid to stir the silt in that pool if I don't have to. Keep the peace.

If Addy doesn't come over, maybe we'll have a quiet night tonight. I love walking into the quiet house, Jack napping on the couch. It's our own version of the deep dark quiet. I kiss him awake and he stirs and wipes his eyes just like when he was a boy. We move around in our own quiet for a while and when we're settled I put on a record or sometimes let him choose one for us. He always goes for the saddest songs, Billie Holiday, or Aretha singing the blues, but it doesn't feel sad when we're all together, it's so lovely. I'll start dinner and listen for the front door, the rattle click and swoosh and in comes Colleen, then Mary, then James, and they all fooster around in the front closet with their coats and come around to the stove to kiss me one by one by one and we're all together, me like a queen cooking and all the quiet sounds of home swimming around me, and, *This is family*, I think and I am happy, and not even Addy can convince me otherwise and even she knows it, otherwise why else would she come over all the time? It's not just for James and surely not just for the food, it's for dinner with us, with our family, and I shouldn't be so selfish. She's lonely and I'm happy to ease her loneliness, otherwise maybe she'd be even more miserable and who'd be able to stand her then. It's fun at home and she wants to be part of it. Some nights, depending on what's on the record player, Colleen will sing along or add her own riff in between and Mary and Jack'll dance the dishes to the table and it's like living in a circus, all the clowns twirling and dancing like mad getting ready for dinner. But you can't do that all the time or it'd get silly.

So many of the houses around here small and sad and unkempt and how can people live like this, and this is my neighborhood? And where was the point it all changed? But at least our block is clean and has good people. *Go around! Don't rush me! Jesus!* I'd pull off and sleep a bit, but I'm so close. Step it up and I can get there faster. Roll down the window, let in some fresh air. That's it. Keep me alert. Jesus, that wind is freezing. I love the smell of wet cement in the cold. Oh, it's here already, and I didn't even notice. The snow now all white and fluffy and drifty like a dream even though it's coming on thick like this. Snow is quieter than rain, maybe that's why I like it.

Okay. Be almost home when I see that big old tree standing steady like ancient Methuselah at the end of the street, tree limbs like arms stretched out wide to welcome me home, then after that just a few more blocks down our tree-filled, pretty street into the dark hush of home, and open the door and smell that smell like no other home. It smells like us, it hits you right when you first walk in, just for a second then it's gone. I wonder what it is, our skin, our sweat or cooking or soap or I guess all of it all together all five of us. I wonder if that smell would change if someone left. Maybe when the kids leave I'll know. No, I can't bear to think about that, I love it the way we are right now when it's just us five all quiet. I hope that's how it'll be tonight, I like that best, the music playing softly, something foreign or with no words and everyone moving silently table to cupboard to dishwasher to me to James at the table doing his crossword and all is my deep quiet except for the squeak and poomph of cupboards opening and closing, the soft rattle of plates unpacked from shelves, the ever so slight clack and tinkle of knives and forks and glasses and plates on the tabletop while I stir the sauce on the stove and in a nearby pan there's the whispering bubble of meat basting and the smell of it filling the whole house, and maybe on a night like tonight the snow hushing down around the house. Colleen will fix the salad for me and even with my back to the room I can hear the splash of water over the lettuce, the whirr of the water circling before the suck of the drain, the slicing swish of a knife through a tomato, Mary's bracelets clinking, and Jack *shush shush shushing* his slippers over the floor, and when I turn from the stove and see them all moving silently back and forth weaving in and out and around one another all hushed no need to talk or sing or dance, just everything quiet and comfortable everyone silent in their own skin and moving back and forth around the kitchen no one matters in the whole world just us, and then when everything's ready we all drift and settle into our rightful places at the table as if that's the way it was when time began and that's the way it'll be forever and ever amen.

Ah, Methuselah. Wipers go *wisp, wisp, wisp, wisp.* Quiet, *wisp, wisp,* dark, *wisp,* then, soon, home.

Acknowledgments

Thanks to Joseph Olshan and all the staff at Delphinium Books for their insight, intelligence, and diligence that made this book come alive.

I owe a great debt of gratitude to the Michener-Copernicus Society of America, an Alice Sheets

Grant, and a Houghton Mifflin Literary Fellowship, all of which provided essential financial support during the writing of this novel.

I would like to thank the editors at the literary magazines where some of these chapters first appeared for their patience, guidance, and generosity: J.L. Torres and Aimee Baker at *Saranac Review*, Brigid Hughes at *A Public Space*, Toni Graham at *Cimarron Review*, Alfredo de Palchi at *Chelsea*, and Clint McCown at *Beloit Fiction Journal*.

Many, many, many thanks to a few of the many people who helped foster the development of this book: Connie Brothers, Frank Conroy, Olena Kalytiak Davis, Darleen Lev, Elizabeth McCracken, Molly McNett, Marilynne Robinson, Deb West, Jan Zenisek, and all the writers at the Iowa Writers' Workshop who saw the first glimmerings of these characters.

And for absolutely everything, I thank Derek Fox.

About the Author

Joseph O'Malley's short fiction has appeared in such magazines as *Glimmer Train*, *Cimarron Review*, and *A Public Space*. He is the author of a collection of short stories entitled *Great Escapes from Detroit*. He was born in Detroit and lives in New York City.